New ⎯⎯⎯⎯
Tales and the *Sam and Hollis* mysteries!

Marianna Trench is an expert at delivering bad news.

For the right price, she'll deliver yours.

Unemployed and dangerously near the last of her savings, Marianna Trench makes a deal that will change her life. After a career of chasing politicians and other crooks, laid-off reporter Marianna knows how to deliver bad news. A spur of the moment favor exchange with a clerk in the unemployment office quickly evolves into a flourishing new business.

At first, it's easy; she's doing good deeds, really. Marianna will break up with your boyfriend without hurting him and leave you looking good. Need to tell off an annoying co-worker? Get a smelly employee to clean up her act? Call Marianna! As her list of happy clients grows, word travels fast of the unusual new service. But bad news has a way of circling back to its source and there's the whole 'kill the messenger' thing.

Set on Maryland's Eastern Shore in the town made famous in the *Sam and Hollis* mysteries, *No Good Deed* is a laugh-out-loud tale of big and little life decisions and the unintended consequences of telling the unvarnished truth to an unsuspecting audience.

~

NO GOOD DEED

HELEN CHAPPELL

No Good Deed

© 2017 Copyright Helen Chappell

ALL RIGHTS RESERVED

For any inquiries regarding this book, please email:

oysterbackpress@gmail.com

Chapter One

"We called the Vandalay Industries number you gave us," the unemployment woman said. "Then we Googled it. You applied for work at a place that doesn't exist." She frowned at me over her glasses, tapping the form with a long black fingernail. Her polish was chipped, I noted idly.

So there I was, at the Watertown unemployment office once again. And once again, I was in trouble. To collect your check in Maryland, you have to fill out a form stating you've applied for work in two different places each week. The trouble is, when you were a reporter for a newspaper that folded up and blew away in the techno age, there aren't a lot of jobs for a woman of a certain age with limited experience.

Experience limited to getting the story, writing it up, fact checking it, fighting with the copyeditor over whether or not the Associated Press Style Manual, bible of journalism, uses proper nouns for job titles in the correctional system, then fight with the editor who wanted the story changed significantly because An Advertiser was involved, and Commandment Number One on a newspaper is "Thou Shalt Not Offend the Advertisers".

All that, then getting it into print, then fielding the angry phone calls from the subject of the story. A great skill set, but not one in high demand. Tourism and selling real estate to retirees make up the industry around here on the Eastern Shore of the Chesapeake Bay. These seemed to be the only career options open to a woman of my age, mid- thirties. Unless I wanted to sign on with a waterman to cut salt eel bait or cull crabs or oysters. I would have preferred this to taking the real estate course at the community college. The trouble with that idea is watermen think a woman on board is bad luck, and it takes a strong back to do the kind of wretched physical labor involved in harvesting the Chesapeake Bay. The tourist- industrial service complex was interested only in young, cute and part time. Becoming a Realtor was looming large and threatening in my future. I'm lousy at sales.

There was office work, but my Microsoft Office skills were rusty, to say the least. Again, offices liked young and cute. That left me off since I hadn't been young and cute in about twenty years.

Real estate was precarious and competitive. And you had to take an enormously hard class and pass an enormously hard test only to watch Chip from Heep and Bingley snatch your client out from under you at the last minute. In an area still coping with property bought high and now desperately selling low, I could end up eating out of dumpsters. In short, once I'd sent a resume to every media outlet in the five- county radius, to be greeted with a resounding silence, it was going to be real estate. I was applying at minimum wage places just to say I had fulfilled the requirements for my unemployment.

"Well?" the lady in front of me said impatiently, snapping me back into the present.

"I can explain," I started to say. But the woman, whose nametag said Betty Tiderman, had probably heard it all before. I could tell she was sick and tired of the weary and unemployed and their pathetic excuses in a pathetic economy.

"My supervisor is a Seinfeld fan," Name Tag Betty continued, unamused. "Do you think you're the first client who ever tried that on us?"

I had the grace to look ashamed. "I've run out of places to apply," I admitted. "Look, I'm desperate. I've applied at every newspaper and magazine in the state."

"There's always WalMart," Betty pointed out. I must say, she had a talent for the obvious.

"I applied at WalMart. Three

times. Three times they told me I was overqualified. And I dumbed down my application. Took off the college. None of the chains are hiring. Neither is the hospitality industry. Look, just dock me a week and let me go. You know and I know that the Eastern Shore is in the worst shape since the Depression and I'm too old and have too few skills to get hired for anything. They all want young blondes with big boobs. Even the doctor's offices. The resort hotels, the office jobs, no one wants people like me. I'm too worn out to flip burgers. Years on my feet pretty much rule that out."

"Well, I really don't have any choice but to withhold your check this week. Believe me, I don't want to, but then I'd be in trouble. And I need this job." For a minute, Betty was almost human. And I could see her point. A job, even a state contract job with no benefits listening to life's losers was better than nothing.

"I'm not mad at you. I know you don't make the rules." It was a line I'd learned to play out over the years of trying to draw the truth out of people without power, but with knowledge. And it usually worked.

Her cell phone started to vibrate. She looked at the number and frowned. "I gotta take this. We're not supposed to take personal calls at work. Do me a favor and keep an eye out for a bald guy in a green shirt. He's my supervisor-- What is it, Ted?" She sounded really annoyed.

I looked outside the walls of her cubicle. All I saw was despair under fluorescent light. But I kept an ear on her conversation because I'm trained to be nosy.

"Ted, I'm not supposed to take personal calls at work. I've got someone here. No, I'm not free tonight. Going to the sports bar with you and your friends Saturday night? Shoot some pool? What you mean is I get to sit with your friend's friends' bimbo girlfriends, who I barely like, while you and your buddies shoot pool and drink cheap beer. Yes, that's what will happen. No, it won't be any diff- - - No. I don't want to go to the

MMA tournament. Why can't we get some tickets for the Shorebirds or go to the beach or . . ." I spotted the bald guy with the green shirt coming down the aisle. He looked like nine miles of bad road. I wouldn't want to be at his mercy. And he didn't look to me like a Seinfeld fan. He looked pretty humorless.

"Super-visor al-ert." I coughed. Not too obvious or anything.

"Gotta go." Betty shut down her phone just as Bad Boss came to her cubicle. He looked at me like I was something he'd scraped off his shoe. "Vandalay Industries?" he snapped.

I nodded cheerfully. "I wanted to be a latex salesman," I said. They were already docking me a week's unemployment, which I couldn't afford. Why not go for the gold?

He glared at both Betty and me, then rumbled on leaving a trail of what my dad called shiny ass bureaucrat syndrome in his wake.

I looked at Betty and she looked at me. We both shrugged. Suddenly, we were in this together. I'd taken a hit for her, and she knew it.

"Thanks," she said. "He's a real stickler for the rules. We call him Little Putin."

"Can't argue with that."

Suddenly, she did the last thing I was expecting. She took off her glasses and began to wipe tears from her eyes. "I can't stand it anymore," she whispered. "I just can't stand it."

"Oh, he's just an ass. I've had editors who would cook me and eat me if they could." I dug around in my pocketbook for some Kleenex.

"Oh, not Wilcox. My boyfriend Ted. I just can't take it anymore."

"If he's abusing you, I've got a list of people and places you can call. I was a reporter. I've got all kinds of contacts. . ."

She put up a hand, waving it from side to side. "No, he'd never lay a hand on me. He's the nicest guy you'd ever want to meet. I should feel so lucky

to have him, but I don't. He's just so. . . "
She waved her hand, conveying miles of
woman-to-woman meaning. "Boring.
Useless. You know, you date a string of
losers, and you finally settle for a nice
guy. And you think your troubles are
over. But you're wrong. Ted is a loser.
He lives in his mother's basement with
his Star Trek collection. He doesn't have
a clue. I don't expect George Clooney
and hearts and diamonds, but it just turns
out that he'd rather hang with his friends
down to the sports bar or play video
games than oh, I don't know, go to a
movie, out to dinner, to a concert.
Anything but sitting there drinking warm
beer and watching him play pool with
his buddies. He doesn't know how to do
anything else and he's not going to
change." I handed her a Kleenex and she
blew her nose.

"You can't change people," I
said. "I'm older than you. I know. I've
seen them all. He'll always pick his
mother over you, or it's just one more
thing before he'll commit, or he's always
going to leave his wife and never
does..."

Betty nodded. "That's exactly right! I used to think, you know, that I was nothing without a man. But I've settled so many times, I'm beginning to wonder what it would be like just to be me and single. "

"A whole world of possibility," I said, feeling wise. Every relationship I'd ever been in tanked. What did I know but being on my own? Maybe if I'd settled for a loser or a married man or a drunk, I'd be not alone. Lonely, but not alone. I shook that thought right out of my head.

Betty twisted the Kleenex in her hands. "I'm sorry. I know you've got your own problems. It just hit me all of a sudden. I want out of this relationship and I have for months."

"Then get out. And don't worry about my problems. I'll survive." I would too, but you don't tell Unemployment about your off the books job, even if it's chump change. "Just break up with him. If you do it while he's trying to sink a ball in the right pocket, he won't even notice."

"I can't. I just can't bear to face him. He's a nice guy. I'm afraid I'll hurt him. And it's really not his fault. We're just not meant for each other. If he'd just finally move out of his mother's house and get a real job. . . and pay his child support without me having to bail him out. . ."

I didn't even know the guy and I wanted to track him down and kick ass and take names. She did deserve better. She wasn't a bad person. She just, like me, made bad decisions. That's when it struck me. The idea that would change my life.

"Look, what if I broke up with him for you?" I blurted out. "Gimme his number, I'll meet up with him and tell him it's you, it's not him. I can do this. What else do I have to do? I've been out of a job for eight months."

"You'd do that?"

"I'd do that. I'll do anything short of homicide. 'Ted, I'm sorry, but Betty wants to break up with you. It's not you, it's her. She thinks you want different things in life, and while you're a terrific guy, you're terrific for someone else, not her. She needs some time on her own.' Look, stories are what I do for a living. I have no investment in him. He'll come away thinking it was his idea."

Betty blinked and put her glasses back on. She leaned in toward me. "You do this for me, I'll make that hold on this week's unemployment check go away."

"You've got a deal."

We shook hands on it. Her chipped black nails and my bitten down stubs. Sisterhood is powerful.

And in the back of my mind I'm thinking, this will make one hell of a story. I just didn't know it was just the beginning of a much, much longer tale.

Chapter Two

"Thanks for agreeing to meet me," I said to the bony redhead as he slid into the booth. "You're Ted, right?"

He nodded. He was about thirty and still wearing his baseball cap backwards and indoors. A scruffy goatee tried to grow from his chin, and I wasn't especially impressed with the beginnings of a poorly executed tat sleeve running up his left arm. Also, he smelled like x Body Spray and he needed dental work.

Unemployment Betty, I decided, could do better. The deciding factor was the tee shirt advertising Big Pecker's Bar and Grill in Ocean City. I really couldn't bitch about him hanging out in the middle of the day, jobless, since I was pretty much in the same boat.

"So you wanted to see me? What for?" Ted asked. His eyes never rested on me, but kept looking at his buddies at the pool table in the corner. Overhead, a mute TV broadcast an old Baltimore Ravens game.

That he didn't seem surprised a perfect stranger had called a meeting with him should have been my first clue. A staggering lack of curiosity is often a sign of a dim mind. Oh, Betty, you could do a whole lot better.

I did get a curious look from the slatternly waitress who slammed two longnecks down in front of me, for which I paid. Ted seemed used to women picking up his tab because he didn't even bother to thank me as he raised a bottle to his lips and drained off about half the beer in one gulp. "If it's about my truck, I told the guy on the phone, as soon as I get my tax return, I'll catch up my payments."

I took a deep swallow of my own beer. I was going to need something to fortify myself for the job ahead. Delivering bad news was going to be unpleasant. Ted might be a clueless unemployed redneck, but he had feelings.

"Actually, Ted, it's not about your truck," I said slowly. What had seemed like such an easy job back at the unemployment office now loomed full of horrible possibilities. What if he started crying? Threatened to kill himself? Jumped off the Bay Bridge? Blamed me for it? Why didn't Betty grow a pair and do this herself? I reminded myself that my weekly check lay in the balance and put on my big girl panties to deal with it.

"The thing is, Betty wants to break up with you. And she asked me to do it because she doesn't have the heart to tell you herself. It's not you, it's her. She just doesn't think she's good enough for you. She thinks you deserve someone who- - - someone who can treat you the way you deserve to be treated."

While I sat there watching this speech slowly absorb into his beer-soaked consciousness, I thought what this loser deserved was a blow to the back of the head, a quick roll up in an old piece of used wall-to-wall carpet, duct tape and a trip to the dumpster behind Food Lion. His focus was still on the pool table. Clearly, I'd dragged him away from his one and only true love, billiards. And maybe his video came in a close second.

"Betty wants to do what?" he asked, dragging his attention back from the 8 ball in the corner pocket.

"Betty," I repeated slowly and clearly, "Is breaking up with you. She asked me to do it. She can't face doing it herself, because she doesn't want to hurt you. It's not you. It's her."

He grudgingly turned to face me. "Betty wants to break up with me?" I noticed he had a big black cavity in his right incisor. Lovely. Ted was one of life's little losers and he was too dumb to know Betty might not have been red carpet material, but she was too good for him,

"Like I say, she didn't want to tell you, so she sent me, because she didn't want to hurt you face to face. This is just killing her, you know. She really feels you're too good for her, and she needs to let you go so you can pursue your dreams."

Which as far as I could tell, was to hang out, drink beer, and play Black Ops and pool 24-7. If he had a job, I had no idea what it was. Betty hadn't mentioned gainful employment.

Ted pondered this, his brow furrowing. After a moment, he said, "Does this mean she don't want the money back? I know I said I borrowed it, but it was really a gift, at least until I get my tax returns."

Betty hadn't said anything about money. I hoped she'd consider it the cost of life experience. "I'm sure you can forget about the money." I lied blithely, peeling the label off my wet beer bottle.

He grinned craftily. He was cunning, in the way uneducated and unintelligent people are, crafty and dishonest. "I guess my wife will be glad to know it's over," he laughed. "I wasn't lookin' forward to tellin' Betty about Misty. And the kids."

I just sat there, gobsmacked.

Whiskey Tango Fox? This guy was a bigger loser than even I thought.

"What were you gonna tell Misty about Betty?"

Ted shrugged. "Nothin'. What she don't know won't kill her. Tell her and the whole trailer park knows."

He downed the rest of his beer. "Hey, that's my quarter on the table, Critter! I'm up next!" he called across the bar.

"Well, then git your ass over here, Mofo!"

"I gotta go. But I gotta thank you, lady. You really done me a big favor. Betty was getting to be a drag. She wanted a commitment, and one old lady and a couple a kids is enough for me. Ted's man enough for more than one lady, but I can do better than Betty!" He wiped his hand across his lips. "What are you doin' tonight, baby doll?"

"Having a shower and a douche and washing my hair and taking an enema and cleaning out every other body orifice before I scrub myself down with bleach."

"Too bad. You and I could do some serious rock and roll together, Babe."

As I was walking out, I noticed a guy sitting alone at the bar. He was nursing a drink and reading something on a Kindle and he wasn't half bad. Handsome in a kind of Harrison Ford way, graying at the temples, a little weather-beaten around the edges. When he grinned at me, I started to grin back.

"You must feel really good about yourself, lady," he said. "Going around breaking people's hearts."

"I'm doing a favor for a friend," I raised an eyebrow. "And this concerns you because?"

He laughed. He had a nice laugh. "Kind of like a reverse wingman. Breaking up for people who don't have the guts to do it themselves. How's that feel? I don't know if you're brave or stupid."

"Tell your significant other to give me a call when she gets tired of your act," I replied, flipping him the cheap business card I'd had made up when I still thought I could get a new job. I didn't look back to see what he did with it.

Safe in my car, in the parking lot, I put my head on the steering wheel. "Betty," I said aloud. "You dodged a bullet."

Or I took it for you. The smell of Axe Body Spray lingered in my nostrils. I knew it would take forever to go away.

Chapter Three

Wednesday night, I was in the office at the staff meeting of *The Santimoke Gazette*

Which is to say I was at a corner table at the Lucky Duck Brew Pub with my fellow ex-employees, drinking designer beer and chewing up my weekly cheeseburger and fries. Present and accounted for were Stu, our former managing editor and present Fearless Leader, who bore a strong resemblance to Groucho Marx. Jimmy; once and future sports editor, who looked rumpled and like the husband and daddy of many kids; Donna, erstwhile business and community reporter, slender, lovely, fine-boned strawberry blonde. And then me, not so lovely and not-so-talented reporter formerly known as features department. This had been our table every payday when the paper was alive.

Now that we were trying to pull together a fledgling online newspaper, our Wednesday table at the Duck was our office. So far, Dickie, the bartender hadn't tossed us out, and as long as we drank up, ate up and paid up at last call, we were free to stay there like a pack of Bolsheviks plotting our next revolution. We should have been plotting the next issue: all our laptops were open and the Wi-Fi was free, but I had to relay my weird experience to the crew. Anything to avoid actually working until the very last minute.

"So, my check was in the mail," I was saying, Ted is gone from Betty's life, and my job search continues. "After I ran the tape about the scene at the pool hall over and over in my head for about twenty hours, I realized I actually pulled it off. He didn't kill me, he didn't cry, and Betty is a free woman."

I didn't bother to mention the smartass guy at the bar. Life was too short to be bothered with fools, especially ironic, oddly attractive fools who were probably married and hung out at a pool hall.

The Lucky Duck, located downtown in Courthouse Square, attracted a slightly more upscale clientele. I'm sure you've seen one of these local pubs in your travels. Places with exposed brick walls and antique mahogany bars. This being the Chesapeake Bay, the décor was waterfowl. Decoys and bird carvings of dubious antique provenance, repro Audubons and local landscape artists specializing in boats, barns and birds. It was just like the inside of Roger Tory Peterson's head. Which suited the clientele just fine.

The white collar of Watertown gathered at this watering hole. Mostly lawyers, since it was opposite the courthouse, but let's not forget the Realtors, the financial advisors and the ladies and gentlemen of the medical profession. All of them came here to socialize, sample the microbrews and chow down on the thick burgers and hefty crab cakes that were the backbone of the menu. Bird theme, hence the

Lucky Duck.

If the pool hall was the home of crabbing news, the Duck was the place where the wheeling and dealing and business of the county was carried out. A smart reporter could drift in and out of both environments without attracting too much attention. But now the Duck was where we hopeful few met to connect and conspire.

My off-the-books secret reporter job wasn't much, but it scraped an extra few bucks into my budget every week. What do most laid-off reporters do? They start a blog and hope the advertisers can support them. It had seemed like a good idea at the time.

It had gone down like this: One fine day without warning, a woman in a too tight suit with a too tight facelift and helmet hair, accompanied by two lugs, marched into the newsroom. "May I have your attention, please?" she called.

We were all on deadline, so most of us didn't pay attention until she banged on the copier.

"I'm from the head office in Charlotte. I regret to tell you, this newspaper is no longer profitable, and we are closing it down. Your severance checks will be in the mail. You have fifteen minutes to clean out your desks and leave. Thank you."

"That's the Hatchet Woman," someone muttered. "They send her out to fire people and close down papers. She's evil."

And that was how dead tree media left Watertown. No more local daily with local news.

Three or four of us gathered at the bar after cleaning out our desks. A glum, if defiant silence settled over us as it sank in we were unemployed. No one was surprised the paper folded. It was more a matter of when than how. This is how technology changes the world, not with a whimper, but a bang. We wouldn't miss Cluthulu, our publisher, who had been reassigned to run another newspaper into the ground.

Sure we could have whined

about bad management, poor decision making, covering up the peccadilloes of the important citizens, the abysmal political bias, but it didn't matter. In the age of electronic media, dead tree journalism was as extinct as the dinosaurs. Now instead of picking up the paper every day, people read the news online and got it the scraps from the radio station. Ad revenues had dropped like a suicide off the Bay Bridge. The chain cut and cut and cut until they couldn't cut anymore, then beheaded the survivors, took a huge tax loss and bought the owner a third new bunker in St. Maarten.

First world problems, I know. But still.

So, after a couple or three drinks on that black day, we decided to start up our own online newspaper. Of course! Brilliant! The county still needed a newspaper, we were obviously social misfits who were unequipped for the real world, and with our pitiful severance checks uncashed, we were feeling white trash rich. Did I mention we were also a little drunk?

Yeah, that too.

That was five months ago. It seemed like a good idea at the time, but it wasn't quite working out the way we'd hoped. *The Santimoke Gazette* debuted to a public not exactly clamoring for local news, even if it was free and online. We were supporting ourselves with a little advertising and we were all collecting unemployment just to make ends meet.

Since the blog could count as employment, even though we were each taking home about $25 a week, we had to keep our involvement quiet. So the need for no bylines was imperative. Besides, now that we were writing what was really going on, rather than what didn't offend the advertisers, we didn't want to be lynched.

Still, Glack's Good Oil and Gas, Lester's Ford Mazda and Tracy's Floral Designs were each willing to dole out a small amount of money each month to sponsor *The Santimoke Gazette.* So far, we were offering it for free once a week. As long as we didn't diss fossil fuels, Fords, Mazdas and flowers, we were okay.

My job was to write the community news. I shared covering local news with Stu and was transferring several wedding announcements and an obituary from my email into my copy folder as we met.

"Just let you break the news to her boyfriend," Stu mused. "Just deliver my bad news and I'll let you off the hook." He peered at me over his glasses. "Marianna, you're the new Hatchet Woman."

"That would make a great column." Donna took a fry off my plate and ate it. Since she weighed as much as a feather, she could get away with it. I didn't even dare finish the serving.

"It's a great story," Jimmy agreed, shaking his head. "But you write that, and we're all screwed."

Donna shrugged, her curls bouncing. "No one would believe it anyway. Nobody believes that the old Bascomb place actually sold. And for half a mil at that." She looked at her reporter pad. "Celia Garth sold it to some retirees from Silver Spring. She's taking a month off and going to Paris. I told her, her real estate company ought to throw a little advertising our way, so maybe they will. We could use the extra income. Of course, then I'd have to run a bought and sold sidebar on the real estate section once a month, but that practically writes itself. Every Realtor in town will be letting me know what's happening. It's mostly press releases anyway this week. The VFW is handing out scholarships, the AAUW named their new officers, that kind of stuff. I can fill twenty, thirty inches this week with that stuff."

"The Oysters won the lacrosse game this week, the Lady Rockfish lost to Devenaux County. . . I've got about twenty inches of local sports. And two more games this week, plus photos."

"Keep it up. A lot of our readers check in just for the local sports," Stu said around a mouthful of burger. "Maybe we can get some of the businesses who sponsor the teams to kick in some advertising for the pages. We've got to get more revenue coming in."

If he sounded wistful, he probably was. Everyone but me was married with a working spouse bringing in at least some kind of income. Of course they had kids and mortgages, too. If this experiment didn't work, we were all screwed, but the way I saw it, they were more screwed than me. My family had all moved to Florida. I was the last one still living in the old hometown.

I could pull up my roots and go down there and find something, even if I ended up as a sea hag, tending bar in some fisherman's dump on the wrong end of the Keys. I knew I'd probably never get out of here, but it was a nice escape fantasy. I was pretty sure our little e-paper was a fool's errand. We only had about 500 readers, but we were also the only source of local news. Even the radio didn't have reporters. And as pessimistic as I felt some days, I was damned if I was going to be the one to puncture our one last gesture of defiance. I loved the Eastern Shore. This is where I'd grown up, where my roots were. Some days when things were especially bleak, packing a few things into a suitcase and running like crazy didn't seem like a bad idea. Other days, when I was a short a dollar at the grocery store and was told to bring it next time, or needed to borrow someone's swimming pool, I felt pretty good about my roots here. I had to give it one more chance.

"These things take some time," Stu said as he did at the end of every editorial meeting. He hit a button and all of our stories copied into his laptop. He would do the layout, such as it was and put it up online tomorrow.

As I did at the end of every Wednesday night, I felt tired, discouraged. It was one of those days when running away and starting a new life seemed like a good idea. That the paper wasn't going well and I wasn't in the mood to call a friend or go to a movie or even get out the kayak and paddle down the river shore in the long summer dusk. I felt lonely and afraid. If I couldn't write, I really had no purpose.

Chapter Four

I was halfway down the darkened street, zig-zagging toward my car when my phone buzzed in my pocket. No one ever calls me at night. I pressed the button, a little annoyed. "Yeah?" I asked, avoiding a tipsy couple locked in a teenage smooch under a streetlight.

"Is this Marianna Trench?" An unfamiliar male voice asked.

"You've got her. What can I do for you?"

"This is Finn McCall. We met at the pool hall the other day. You were giving the brush-off to some guy so his girlfriend didn't have to do it?"

"That's pretty much what happened," I agreed, cheering up just a little. A call from an interesting guy! "Who can I dump for you?"

He laughed. "You're feisty. I like that in a woman."

"You talk like someone in a bad romance novel. That annoys me no end in a man."

A cool breeze was blowing down the street. The clock in the courthouse was chiming. "Get to it," I said. "I turn back into a beautiful princess in about thirty seconds."

I knew he wouldn't get it and he didn't. "Let me get to the point. I have a job that needs someone else to take care of it. Apparently, you deliver bad news."

My mental tumblers clicked together. Think fast, Trench. "I am the Hatchet Woman. For a price, I axe your problem. Who do you want to break up with?"

He laughed. "Oh, it's nothing like that. I can break off my own relationships, thank you. It's something worse. If you have the guts to do it."

I stiffened. He was challenging me, and if there's one thing I don't like, it's someone girly-girling me to do something. I straightened my spine.

"What is it? I don't kill people, at least not this week."

"It's almost that bad, but not quite. And it's going to need some tact and diplomacy, which I'm not sure you have. Some sensitivity. I have a hunch beneath that hard crusty shell, there's a hard crusty heart. But this requires some kindness."

"What is it?"

He took a deep breath. "I need you to tell someone in my boatyard they need to take a bath and use a deodorant."

"Wow." I breathed. "A boatyard. That guy must really stink."

"Worse. It's a woman."

***

Spruce Boatworks was an upscale operation. It covered about three acres down on the Santimoke River toward the Bay, buildings punctuated by high masts of sailboats and enormous fiberglass power yachts up on the stands. More boats floated at the docks. It was the kind of boatyard that catered to people with money to burn. And it was known far and wide as one of the last places that built and serviced quality wooden boats. To say you had a Spruce was a signal you had arrived in Boating World.

A busy, prosperous place, I judged, wandering through the gravel parking lot in search of one of the work sheds where Finn said I could find him.

Inside the open shelter, it was slightly cooler. In the middle of the shed, the ribs and keel of a wooden hull filled the room like a giant wooden skeleton. It was graceful, the design of someone who knew and understood wooden boats. Two men were working on laying in the planking, while a third man worked with the wood steamer, bending flat oak boards into a convex shape.

Through the steam, I could barely make Finn out, but I noted he was bare-chested, naked from the waist wearing only a pair of heavy welders' gloves as he pushed himself against the wood planking. I hadn't gasped like that at a man's chest since I absent- mindedly picked up that issue of Vanity Fair with a shirtless Rob Lowe on the cover.

Yeah, that was some eye candy, and it was Finn his ownself. Years of heavy physical labor had accomplished what no gym could do. From his neatly cut arms to his muscular chest to the flat abs and the hair that nestled in the middle of his chest and descended into his well-worn jeans, he was pretty breathtaking.

It took me a moment to compose myself. If I'd been in a Jane Austen novel I would have been one of those secondary characters who has a fit of the vapors and collapses on the chaise longue. But I'm not in a Jane Austen novel, so I took a couple of deep breaths, shook myself back into sanity and gingerly approached the steamer. You don't want to stand too close to those things. That vapor can burn you.

I also know how rude it is to break someone's concentration, so I stood patiently in his line of sight waiting for him to notice me. Besides, it was nice to just stand there and admire the view. For a guy who was probably in his late 30s, he was looking just fine. Slowly, I was distracted by something other than the intoxicating aroma of cedar and milled oak. Something with bottom notes of heavy death, middle notes of funk and shrieking top notes of eau de armpit. It was as bad as Finn had said, and it was out to get me.

Out of the corner of my eye I saw one of the guys working on the boat's planking was actually a girl, and when she moved closer to me, I realized she was the source of the stink. She was thin but sturdy, and hefting those boards like they were made from cotton. When she lifted her arms, I saw she didn't shave, which was her business not mine, but if you don't clean out your pits now and then, that hair tends to make them noisome. She was wearing a tank top, shorts and heavy socks with work boots, and had a bandanna tied over her hair, pirate style. The universal boat worker outfit.

Not that you expect anyone working in a yard on a hot day to smell heavenly, even if they shower every night, but Finn was right. This was something special.

I was surprised because in my experience, women tend to be more aware of personal hygiene than men. She didn't look like one of those girls who never quite got over that whole 60s organic thing. She simply reeked.

What surprised me was that she was very pretty. Dark, with brown eyes and black hair and, to me, looked Native. Someone touched my arm, and I turned. I found myself staring at blonde chest hair. "Come with me," Finn said, gesturing toward a door. "I don't want anyone to see you here."

I could barely hear him over the noise of power tools, but I followed him through a door and into another building, where he seemed to have an office buried under a ton of paperwork, wood, tools, Ridgid Tool calendars and clutter. Somewhere he found a desk under all that debris and cleared a stack of *Wooden Boat* off a chair for me.

He sat down, wiped his face with a bandana and leaned back. "Better if no one notices you too much," he grunted. From a tiny refrigerator hidden somewhere, he pulled out a couple of cans of soda and passed me one. The cold liquid felt good in the heat. "See, I've given this some thought. There are a couple of things going on here. First, I don't think anyone working here needs to confront someone about a B.O. problem. At the end of a hot day, we all stink like a troop of baboons in heat. But usually at the beginning of next day, we come in pretty cleaned up. But when someone just plain stinks, day after day, to the point where my crew notices a problem, and we're talking about a bunch of guys here, then something's got to be done."

"Understood," I said. "It is a delicate situation. I've been thinking about it. No one wants to bring bad, humiliating news like 'Hey, you smell like a corpse flower!' to someone you have to work with. That's where I come in. I seem to be good at delivering bad news." I shrugged wryly, not half as confident as I was feeling.

"Well, that's the second problem. Susan Korsakov's the only woman in the outfit, so that makes it sensitive. She's a great worker and a nice lady. Everyone likes her, and some of us even feel a little protective of her because she's so small. But believe me, she can hold her own. I've seen her pick up a fifty- pound sandbag and swing it over her head like it was a down pillow. Finding people who can still build wooden boats isn't that easy. Everything is fiberglass these days, but people who can pay for it like the old craft."

"Are you afraid she'll slug you for calling her less than dainty?"

Finn grimaced. "Less than dainty doesn't begin to cover it. Look, I was married, I was the only son with four sisters and one bathroom. Lady issues don't bother me. Guys can smell like Peruvian jungle rot, too. I can handle that. It's not a lady problem. It's a soap and water and deodorant problem. But Susan. Well, there's sexual harassment issues, and worse, there's the problem of the guys and the customers not wanting to be around her. I can't tell her she stinks. None of the guys can tell her she stinks. It would humiliate her, and worse, she might quit, and I don't want to lose a worker who can polish teak and run a jitterbug the way she can. So, what can you do for us?" He leaned back, put his heavy boots up on the desk and crossed his arms behind his head. Behind him, I saw a pristine white robe.

"Someone graduating?" I asked.

He followed my gaze. "No, that's my choir robe. I sing in the Men's Choir at St. Luke's A.M.E. Church in Watertown. I'm a pretty decent baritone."

I must have been staring at him because he shrugged and leaned forward in his chair. "They're very welcoming at St. Luke's even of a Whitey McWhite like me. I like the church and I love gospel music. You okay with that?"

I guess he caught some flack about attending a mostly African American church, but I was just fascinated by the fact that he went to church at all. For once in my life, I didn't have a smart crack to make. I admired him because the times I'd been at St. Luke's, I'd enjoyed the music and the warm welcome. It was the polar opposite of what I'd been raised in, and God, without irony knows, a lot more pleasant than say, the all-white Church of the Angry Jesus. Discovering he was a person of faith, any faith at all, cast him in a different light. Just one I couldn't quite figure out.

For a split second, I forgot about Susan's problem and pondered this reminder that people are rarely what you expect them to be. But I quickly snapped back into professional mode.

"This is a delicate mission. I need to think it over. Can you give me 24 hours?" I asked.

Finn shrugged. "Not a minute more. I've got a rebellion stewing in the shop, and I'm afraid one of these macho lugs will say something. You know, some men are meaner than those mean girls everyone talks about."

He swung his feet off the desk and stood up. "Tide and steam bending wait for no man. If I don't get back to work, I'll have one expensive, warped piece of wood that will make a good bonfire. You've got my number. And 24 hours."

"That's all I need," I lied through my teeth. Actually, I had no idea what I was going to do, or how I got myself into this mess. I didn't even know how much to charge.

Chapter Five

S talking people is not that hard. I'd stalked a sneaky politician or two in my day, usually to some No Tel Motel in the next county. Once I'd followed a politician all the way to Annapolis to surprise him taking a cash stuffed envelope from a lobbyist. In a parking lot. But telling someone they smell? That takes a whole level of toughness I wasn't sure I had.

All I had to do was wait at the gate of Spruce Boatworks around quitting time, cleverly hidden from the departing workers by overgrown shadbush. It was a nice June day, not too hot, so waiting wasn't unbearable.

Susan had a battered old Volvo wagon, black beneath a layer of dust. I watched as she turned toward town. Interestingly enough, she had Alaska tags.

"Well, we're a long way from home," I murmured, letting a couple more trucks slide past me before I turned in the same direction Susan'd gone.

We went down the road and she pulled into a gas station. I idled on the other side of the pumps as she went in the ladies' room. She was in there so long I listed to two cycles of news, weather and sports and a full playlist of classic alt rock on the radio. About twenty people went in and out of the convenience store before her.

When she came out, I noticed she was carrying a plastic bag. She got into her car, made a U-turn on the street and headed down the road toward the strip mall on the outskirts of town. At rush hour, the parking lot was busy, but I was able to follow her around WalMart and into the overgrown landscaping around a containment pond.

It was deserted back there, save for some muskrats and a couple of resident geese. A pine forest they hadn't cut down for more development blocked it from general view. She parked the

Volvo behind a dumpster and looked around before she got out of the car and walked to the edge of the pond. There, she sat down and took some lunch meat and bread from a bag, and popped the tab on a Mountain Dew. I watched in my car from a distance as she ate, tossing bits of bread to the geese, which gobbled them up eagerly. I'd never seen Canada geese get so close to a human before. They were practically eating from her fingers. That made me like her. If animals, especially wild animals trust you, it's a sign you're a good person.

I parked the car, grabbed the basket on the passenger seat and headed down the hill. I was careful to sit upwind of her.

"Hi." I ventured casually.

She inched away, eyeing me suspiciously, clutching her sandwich tightly. "Do I know you?" she asked.

"No. My name's Marianna Trench, and you're Susan Korsakov." I kept my voice cheerful and matter of fact. In some ways, she was as wild as the geese and would have bolted just as easily. I smiled, grappling for words. Funny how I never seem to run out of something to say until I need to talk.

This was harder than I thought. Telling someone they stink was suddenly not as easy as it had sounded in my mind. I took a deep breath and pushed the basket between us.

It looked nice if I did say so myself. A wicker basket stuffed with delicious soaps, bath salts, shower gels, shampoos, deodorants and other bath time goodies, all tied with a bright yellow ribbon looked both girly and enticing to me.

Still, Susan inched further away, watching me as if I were about to pull out an axe and have at her there and then. "What do you want?" she asked, narrowing her eyes. "How do you know my name? What's this?"

"Susan," I gulped, and jumped right in. "This is for you." I prodded the basket toward her. "If you look, you can see it's all kinds of great bath stuff. Rose bath salts, Lavender Breeze shower gel,

Fleur de Provence Angelica bath fizzies, four kinds of scented soaps, all kinds of neat stuff. I even threw in some scented candles. It's all for you."

Up close, I could see how thin she was, how delicately boned. She had a smooth olive complexion with huge dark eyes. Her short hair was shaggy and chopped, as if she'd cut it herself. There was a layer of grime in her skin, her pores, her neck. Her nails were black with grime. Up close was unpleasant, to say the least. I stifled an impulse to pick her up and hurl her into the pond with a bar of soap. She might have been strong, but I was bigger and I work out.

She was staring at the basket. Slowly, she reached out with thin fingers and touched the yellow ribbon. "This is for me?"

"For you."

She looked at me from the depths of those chocolate eyes, and I almost burst into tears. She was tougher than me. She blinked. "It's that bad, huh?"

I nodded. "It's that bad. Untie the

ribbon. I picked out this stuff myself from Irma's Tradewinds Boutique, and you know she stocks good stuff."

Susan ducked her head. "I knew I was a little funky, but I didn't know it was. . . "

"Honey, it's bad. You need to bathe more often. When you work a dirty job like that, by the end of the day, even someone who takes a shower every day smells like they've been rolling in old crab shells."

She plucked at the ribbon. "Those guys. This is their idea of a joke, right?"

"They don't have the faintest idea I'm here." Well, it wasn't quite a lie. But the boss isn't one of the guys, no matter what he thinks.

"Then..." She really did look like a deer caught in the headlights, and I didn't blame her. I could tell her reaction was flight or fight, and if she decided to fight me, I wasn't sure I could run fast enough to avoid someone who can heave a fifty-pound sack over her head.

"Let's say I'm your fairy godmother. Now, you need to shower every night in this weather. And use a good deodorant. I've included a Mitchum in there. Doesn't matter if you don't want to shave your pits or your pubes, but you gotta soap 'em up good."

"I guess all those years living in a cabin, you start not to notice your own stink. I guess I got careless. But now, finding a shower isn't that easy. Every once in a while, on pay day, I check into a motel for the weekend."

"Where are you living?"

She clutched the basket against her chest as if she were afraid I'd snatch it away from her. "I live in my car," Susan said. "It's all I can afford. I park in a corner of the boatyard, behind some trailers. It's safer there."

I stumbled to my feet. "First things first. We're gonna get you a hot shower. A bath and a hot shower if that's what you want."

***

While her clothes flipped around in the

dryer, Susan sat on the edge of my couch and dried her hair with one of my towels. She smelled pleasantly of Sandalwood Temple Bath Gel and floral shampoo. You could say she cleaned up good, but I didn't want to add insult to injury. She fairly glowed with the satisfaction of plenty of hot water and scented girly stuff. "Thanks," she told me for about the hundredth time. "I feel so much better. They're pretty sparing with the hot water at the motel. And the gas station bathroom doesn't have hot water."

I know what you're thinking and you're probably right. Inviting imperfect strangers into your home is insane. The way that girl could heft a nail gun, she could probably crucify me against the kitchen wall. But I've got pretty good spider sense, after all those years of being a reporter, and nothing was saying "serial killer" to me.

I selected the next to last piece of pizza from the box and bit into it. The only good thing about my crummy little apartment was that it was right down the street from Carmine's Pizzeria, which is the best in town and delivers. At least we were both getting a hot meal.

On background: I live in what used to be the servant's quarters of one of those grand old houses that line River Street. The two-bedroom apartment is cozy and affordable. My landlady, Mrs. Randolph Tilghman Sharpless, was an elderly widow and a dear family friend who lived in majestic antique-filled splendor. I'd known Miss Wilsie all my life. She had been one of my father's patients before he and my mother retired to Florida, and since I was little I'd adored her as a role model. She was both a grande dame and a great old broad, no mean trick even with a big personality like hers.

But she was also having problems of her own, what with her prig of a son Freddie trying every way he could to get her to move into a nursing home so he could sell this house and get his hands on her considerable money. Right now, Miss Wilsie was downstairs in her library watching Jeopardy or

Wheel of Fortune and for now, she didn't need to know about any of my latest escapades.

River Street is named because it follows the curve of the Santimoke river. In the old days, these splendid old places were the town houses of rich planters who lived out in the country. It was still a pretty street, one that attracts the tourists, even though some of the houses were now a bit down at heel, while others had been restored and gentrified by come-heres who fell in love with the Eastern Shore.

Back to this story. "I'm assuming Finn pays a living wage. Skilled woodworkers are hard to find and a good one can make good money. Why live in your car?" I asked.

She picked up the last slice of pizza, licking the strings of melted cheese off her fingers. "Because if I don't have a permanent address, no one can find me."

"Outstandings? F.T.A.s? Alaska's a long way from here. A whole continent away. And you've got those Alaska tags."

"Outstandings? F.T As?"

She wasn't playing me. I could tell. "Outstanding arrest warrants. Failure to Appear warrants. Are you running from the law?"

She shook her head. "Not from the law. From a man. If he tracks me down, I am sure he'll kill me. He beat the crap out of me the last time I ran. Caught up with me in Seward and made me his punching bag. It was all I could do to get away from him. I emptied out my checking account and drove and drove and drove until I came to the Atlantic Ocean nod I couldn't drive any further. Then I found Spruce Boatworks here and signed on. I worked in boatyards in Alaska and Vancouver.

"But I'm still afraid he'll track me down somehow. And if he does, this time he'll kill me." She spoke matter-of-factly, but she held my interest. I have a good bullshit detector, and I had a feeling she was telling the truth.

"That's why I don't rent a place,

or use my credit cards or stay in a cheap motel more than a couple of nights at a time. Because he can track me. He's clever. So, I wash in cold water in gas station bathrooms, and once a week I shower, and now I'm going to have to move on because I can't go back there and look at the guys knowing they put you up to this."

"Right now, the guys at the boatyard and that crab bait in Alaska are the last things you need to worry about. Finish up the pizza while I make up the futon. You're gonna sleep here tonight, and tomorrow's a new day when we're gonna figure out what the next step is. I tell you one thing. I hate men who abuse women. I used to see a lot of that when I was a reporter, and I hate those scum-sucking pigs like my grandmother hated homemade sin. No one's gonna hurt you on my watch."

At least not until I get to the bottom of this, I thought.

A big part of me thought she was telling the truth, but one thing I learned in journalism. Everybody lies. You just assume it until you can prove different.

But what had I gotten myself into now?

Chapter Six

The rest of the week was quiet. Susan was a good roommate, gone before dawn and back after dark. And with access to a bath, very, very clean. She even did the dishes. I decided it was probably better to leave my landlady, Miss Wilsie, out of the loop for the time being. The fewer people who knew where Susan was, the better.

The next Wednesday, before I left the house for the staff meeting at the Duck, the phone rang. It was a text from one of my brothers, Michael, a professor up in Chestertown at Washington College.

"Sis, there's an opening at the community college in Annapolis for an adult ed writing teacher. You ought to at least apply and finally get out of Watertown. Now that that paper is closed, you need to get across the Bridge and into the real world while you're young enough to get a job. Should have gotten your master's like I told you. Wasting your talent and your life."

And more along those lines. Big Brother's watching me. But still, Michael was an academic, a world so far removed from reality that it may as well be a fantasy film. And he, on his paltry salary as a college professor in a place about the size of Watertown, telling me to teach?

"What," I texted back, "and leave show business and all this behind? FYI, I have a PT job. I deliver bad news for people who don't have the nerve or the style to deliver it in person. And so far, I'm doing pretty well." I typed in the amount of Finn's most generous check and hit send.

That, I thought, ought to travel through the family like electricity on a copper wire. And there would be feedback. What was I up to now? Why couldn't I use my degree and my resume to get a decent job somewhere, make a life for myself that didn't involve living practically rent free with a half-senile old lady, being out of work and involved in yet another harebrained scheme?

If I knew the answer to any of those questions, I'd be wiser than I am.

Year after year went by, and I still clung, like that barnacle on the piling, to what was safe and comfortable. Maybe it was because the one time I'd strayed from the path it had been a disaster. I'd met and married a guy and moved to Manhattan and well, let's just say it didn't work out very well. I crawled home with my tail between my legs and here I stayed, licking my wounds. Sure, there had been other guys, but nothing as heartbreaking as that marriage. Things just didn't work out for one reason or another.

Nonetheless, I copied down the info for Anne Arundel County Community College, because you never know.

Sure enough, as I was combing my hair, my phone buzzed again. It was my other brother, Robert, the successful surgeon at Johns Hopkins who could buy and sell me. I knew within five minutes, I could expect a call from my next-to-me brother Matt, the successful Washington lobbyist. All my brothers had made something of their lives, marriages, kids, while I was the hipster beatnik hippie freak who somehow clung to the old hometown. The baby sister whose different drumbeat no one else in the family heard. To tell the truth, I don't know why I'm still here myself. From time to time, I escaped to live in New York or California or London, but I always came back after a year or so with my tail between my legs. It's hard to be a dreamer.

I turned off my phone, cursed, and walked out the door into a warm June night. The smell of jasmine and sweetbush filled the air of River Street and the houses loomed on either side of the brick walks like grand old sentries.

As I came around the side of the house, I saw Miss Wilsie's light was on and the faint blue TV was broadcasting something. I made a mental note to drop in on her. Usually, we phoned each other once a day, but since we both valued our privacy, we never showed up unannounced.

The Lucky Duck was quiet on Wednesdays. Too early for payday, not close enough to the weekend. So it was just the newspaper crew and a few regulars at the bar, watching men do something with a ball on the overhead TV. Since Main Street was just a couple of blocks from River Street, I usually walked. At that time of night, downtown was pretty dead, except for the bars and restaurants, but it was safe.

I was late when I took my seat and a little breathless. "Welcome to our corner of the universe," Stu said. "So glad you could make it." He hates late. When you spend half your life on deadline, it's like that. "We were planning next week's edition. Do you have your stories ready for editing?" Below his horn rimmed glasses, his mustache twitched. We used to tease him and stay his 'stache was his bullshit detector. But he was in no mood for kidding tonight.

"You have my stories. I emailed 'em last night. And now, you have this."

I pulled my check out and waved it in the air. "I got a little freelance gig. After I paid my rent and some of my bills, I ended up with this. An investment in the Gazette."

Stu looked at the check and his eyebrows rose, making him look more than ever like Groucho.

"Whattya got?" Donna asked, taking it from his limp fingers. "Marianna! Where did you get this kind of money?" Petite and soignée, Donna is everything I'm not. She's also a great mom and one hell of an ad saleswoman. I really admire the way she keeps it all together. If this didn't work out, she'd have to sell real estate. And I'd hate to see that happen. Not that there's anything wrong with it. She'd make a fortune because she's a pleasant person, unlike me.

Jimmy looked at the zeros and whistled. Okay, it wasn't all that great, but for us, it was a small fortune, considering none of us were actually getting more than peanuts to do this little newspaper of ours.

Jimmy was a typical sports guy. Big ginger quarterback. He doted on his wife and kids, and lived to write up the local teams, since he'd been a jock through most of his high school and college career. In his spare time, he was assistant coach on his daughter's soccer team.

"Maybe you'd better tell us how you came by this," Stu suggested, just as the waitress brought my cheeseburger and a Corona. He was laughing, but still.

"Long story short," I began, and went through the thing, just the high points, to keep it interesting. I knew I could trust them not to talk. "I got my unemployment check because I told some idiot his girlfriend was dumping his sorry ass. She didn't have the nerve to tell him herself. Then I've been paid an outrageous sum of money to tell someone they stink. That this person needed to bathe more often. I had no idea there was so much money in delivering bad news."

"Only rich people can afford wooden boats. You can't get insurance on them. They're a status symbol," Donna pointed out. She's an avid sailor, so she knows.

"What a gig!" Jimmy laughed. "You couldn't pay me enough to tell someone they stink, though. That's rough territory. Sounds like this person could haul off and deck you."

"It's a her, to make it more interesting. I always thought men were such slobs, but I was wrong."

"And you say this girl's couch surfing at your place?" Stu asked. All of us are cynics, but Stu is the most suspicious of all. "You don't even know if her story is true, Mar. She could be playing you. Maybe she beat him up in Alaska. I hate to be un-P.C., but a lot of men get beaten up by women, too, you know. Or she could be involved in something even more serious. Did you think to run a check on her record in

Alaska?" Even as he spoke, he was typing into his laptop. Most criminal conviction is public record, and you can find anyone's unsavory past online these days with a search. "What did you say her name was again?"

"Susan Korsakov. A lot of Natives have Russian names because Russia used to own Alaska. But I don't get a hinky feel on her. Well, not too much, not much more than I get on anyone else. She's not going to stay. I made her promise she'd tell her boss the whole story. He's the one who can look after her and he seems to care about her." When I said that, I felt a twinge of regret.

Damn, Finn was attractive. But Susan was young and cute and now, thanks to me, smelled delicious. "I can help her find a place to rent once I convince her some nutcake from Alaska will never find her down here at the jumping off place."

Which is pretty much what the Eastern Shore is. And if the Shore is the jumping off place, Watertown is the waterslide.

Jimmy glanced at his watch. "Can we get this meeting going? I've got to get home early tonight. Got to help Hannah study for her history exam."

I took a big bite of my cheeseburger. One of these days, I really had to start eating healthy. With my free hand, I flipped open my laptop and opened the Gazette file.

"So what have we got for this week?"

Deadlines is deadlines. I shut the phone off and focused on the lead story.

Chapter Seven

When the phone rings that early on a Saturday morning, it means only one thing: my mother is calling from Florida.

"Mari?" Mom's voice cut through my sleep, loud and clear. She still thinks long distance means you have to shout to be heard. "Did I wake you up?"

I rolled over on the cat, who squealed and jumped off the bed in disgust. "No, Mom. I'm always wide awake at 6:45 on Saturday morning."

"Well, I wanted to catch you before you went out. Your father and I have been up since four. We went to Shoney's for breakfast. The senior special. Your father always orders bacon and eggs, even though I tell him he's going to have a heart attack and drop dead on the golf course. Me, I eat oatmeal. I can still fit into my wedding dress. Have you lost that last ten pounds?"

"Mom, let Dad eat his eggs and bacon. The doctor said he's healthier than a horse. We'll both die before he does. Babies being born right this minute will age and die before Dad. He's like a vampire. He's eternal. He only eats eggs and bacon on Saturdays."

Note how I dodged the ten-pound question about the ten pounds.

"So, your brothers tell me you've got some kind of freelance job? Some kind of crazy thing where you tell people off?"

I rolled my eyes. Somewhere, I heard the cat scratching in the litter box. I felt the same way the litter did. "It's not a job. It's just a, a thing."

"Is there money exchanged?"

"Yeah, I get paid. Mom, someone has a piece of bad news they can't deliver for whatever reason, I step in and tell the other person they smell or have bad breath or they're fired or broken up with or, oh, stuff like that."

There was silence between Maryland and Florida. I could feel my mother thinking. And I didn't like it one bit.

"What are people going to say? Your father was an important man in Watertown before he retired. He was Chief of Staff at the hospital. He still gets Christmas cards from former patients. It's been nearly a year since that paper closed. Why don't you get a real job? You know how to use a computer. . ."

"If you ask me why I don't get married again, and let a guy take care of me, I'm hanging up. I haven't had coffee yet, and you know what I'm like un-caffeinated. Besides, you know how well that worked out the first time."

The wind changed quarters, as I knew it would. My parents adored my ex-husband, long out of the picture. I did not. He was the reason I left New York.

"Well, sweetie, since you're doing this freelance bad news bearing, I was hoping you could drop a little hint to your father."

"Isn't that what my brothers are for? I mean they're the respectable ones with the good jobs and the grandchildren and the perfect daughters-in-law." Which was mean, because I do love my brothers, my sisters-in-law and my nieces and nephews. But no coffee and Dr. and Mrs. Russell Trench are not a great combo.

"Well, Mari, it's like this. They were having a rummage sale at the club to raise money for school kids to have food, so I donated a few things Dad and I don't need anymore. It was for a good cause,"

"Not the orange sweater!" I gasped, suddenly wide awake.

My mother sighed. "That sweater is a rag. He's worn it and worn it until there's nothing left for me to patch or darn anymore. It's all repair needlework. Even the tailor in Naples said he couldn't fix it again."

"Mom, does Dad know it's gone?"

"Well, since you're in the bad

news business, I was hoping you'd tell him," my mother said sweetly.

My father had had that sweater for at least twenty years. It was originally a hideous orange, but time, sun and repeated washings had faded it to a sort of creamsicle color. It was a cardigan golf sweater. It was so old and worn out that it looked as if Mr. Rogers had worn it on a weeklong binge and slept in a dumpster in an alley wearing it. It also happened to be my father's lucky golf sweater.

Now I know little about golf and care less, but it's my father's passion, and he swears that sweater makes him a winner on the greens. This is a man of science and rationality, mind you. That sweater is the one thing he's superstitious about. I think he would sooner see us, his family, eaten by wolves than surrender that sweater.

This was serious.

"Mom, can you get it back?"

"That's just it, Mari. It was in such bad shape, the committee wouldn't take it. Mrs. Soforza in Phase Three on the Ninth Hole took it and shredded it to make a braided rug."

I pulled the pillow over my head. "Mom! What have you done? Don't make me tell him! I can't! I just can't. He's my father, for godssake. I can't tell him his lucky sweater has been reincarnated as a rag rug!"

"It was just so ratty. I was embarrassed when he walked out of the house in that thing. All the other golfers laughed about it. To his face."

"Didn't throw the old doctor off his game, did it?"

"No, but I'm afraid without it, he'll lose his edge. What? Oh, Rusty, Mari's on the phone. Say hello to her."

Sotto voce to me: "Break it to him gently, dear."

There was some rustling, I heard my father's deep grumble of protest because he hates, absolutely hates the phone, then in the speaker. "Mari? That you?" He rumbled.

No, Dad, I thought. It's Princess Kate. But I am a daddy's girl, so I tried. "Hi, Dad! Mom called me."

"How are you? Found a job yet?"

"No, but I'm doing some freelance work."

"Good. Want me to send you a check?"

Of course I wanted him to send me a check. Checks are how my father communicates that he loves me and wants me to have food and shelter in hard times. But when he heard what I had to say- - I suppose I could have declined, but my mother is the queen of good Protestant WASP guilt. She would never let me forget I let her down in her moment of crisis. So I took a deep breath.

"Dad, Mom has something she wants me to tell you because she doesn't want to tell you herself."

"What's that?" My old man is nothing if not laconic on the phone. All those years of dinner, sleep and golf interrupted by the ringing of the phone and a patient with an emergency have made him so.

I could almost smell the suspicion.

I took a deep breath. "Dad, Mom threw out your orange golf sweater. She tried to donate it to charity, but it was such a rag they wouldn't take it, so Mrs. Soforza tore it up for a rag rug."

Try getting all of that out in one breath.

There was a horrible, deadly silence on the phone for a few long seconds, then my father bellowed "WHAT?"

"Momthrewoutyourorangegolfsw eatershetriedtodonateitbutheywouldntake itsoMrsSoforzarippedituptomakearagrug."

A stunned, Olympian silence. Then, "LOUISA!"

Then the phone went dead.

Two things. A check came in the mail, and when IslaVista Estates A Gated Community had their silent charity auction, my dad paid a small fortune for Mrs. Soforza's rag rug with the orange braiding, and it rides around on the seat of Dad's golf cart.

It's a tough job, but someone's got to do it.

Chapter Eight

Mrs. Randolph Tilghman Sharpless peered at me over her glasses. "Your father did that?" She asked between bursts of laughter.

"He did. Mom said he paid a lot for that stupid rug. I don't understand golf, but apparently, it's his lucky sweater and takes strokes off his game, whatever that means. And now, it lives in his golf cart. "

Miss Wilsie, as nearly everyone called her, sipped her vodka and held out her glass for a refill. "Freshen yours while you're at it, Mari." As I've noted, she was my landlady, had been a patient of my father's and was someone I'd known all my life. Naturally, she'd been following my new venture with interest, since most of her other friends were elderly club women and stuffy members of the garden clubs and the DAR. When the old servant's apartment in the rear of her stately mansion became available and I was just back from a disastrous stay in London, I'd moved my few sticks of furniture out of my parent's barn and into the_pied a terre. She had a tenant who didn't throw loud college parties and I had a convenient place to crash with a landlady I loved. I was hoping this would be a good time to break the news that I had a temporary roommate, but I was waiting until the vodka made her really mellow.

"So, what do you think?" I asked, handing her a fresh drink. "Is this a bad thing or a good thing, it is a good deed or a bad action? I really need to know if you think this is a good idea."

We were sitting in Miss Wilsie's library, the sunny, least formal room in the house., Miss Wilsie's front mansion was far more elegant than my modest servant's quarters. Generations of Wilsons, Tilghmans and Sharplesses had done pretty well for themselves, and the priceless antiques, export porcelain and

ancestral portraits on every wall proved
it. The place was on every house tour in
the county, and in her own quiet way,
Miss Wilsie enjoyed her position as one
of the Shore's grandest grande dames.
She especially enjoyed striking terror
into the hearts of the pompous and stuffy
of Santimoke County and so a lot of
people were afraid of her, which suited
her just fine. "They don't ask me to
volunteer and they don't ask me for
donations," she winked.

Miss Wilsie leaned back in her
recliner (not an antique) and closed her
eyes. She might have been dragging 89
on a trailer hitch, but she had the fine
bones, flashing eyes and pure white hair
that still made her a beauty.

In her day, my father, who had
known her as a boy when she was a
young woman, told me she had been a
hellraiser. Champion rider and jumper,
competitive, fearless sailor, the first
woman to skipper her own log canoe in
the races, a drinker with a hollow leg,
driving an elegant roadster over the back
roads from one elegant party to the next,

dancing all night, cooking breakfast at dawn for a crowd of adoring young men.

When she finally chose to settle down with Randy Sharpless, it was considered as good as a royal marriage. An alliance of two old bloodlines, people said. Happily, old blood also came well supplied with old money, which is not always the case in these ancient Southern families.

It was sad to me that most of her friends were dead. They sounded like the kind of people I'd find interesting, from a time when being rich on the Shore was actually fun. I'd like to have known Robert Mitchum when he and his family lived here, and tore up and down the river in wooden speedboats, tossing down the booze and raising quarter horses. Miss Wilsie had some old home movie of the Duke and Duchess of Windsor doing the Charleston. Yeah, she'd led that kind of life, and yet she was never snobbish, unless of course, you offended her, and then, look out.

Mr. Randy had died of a sudden heart attack in the bar of the Santimoke

Country Club nearly twenty years ago, and Wilsie missed him dearly, but widowhood didn't curb her enthusiasm for life. "I would have divorced Randy years before he died," she once confided to me in a whisper, "But we were waiting for the kids to die so it wouldn't upset them." She often told the joke, laughed and winked, vastly amused, holding my hand inside her thin, strong fingers. "isn't that wicked?" Age hadn't hurt her grip one bit. Over the years, we'd chatted quite a bit about the old days, when she picked berries and crabs along with the help and all about her horses and her sailing, the amazing people she'd known, the places she and Randy had traveled. She'd had a great life, and she was still enjoying it.

She also had the great gift of treating everyone from several presidents to the trash men with exactly the same friendliness and consideration, which made her one of the most beloved people I knew. Needless to say, I adored her, and managed to keep an eye on her, since she lived alone, except for a housekeeper who came in several times a week to keep the house tidy and make sure her needs were met. Her nurse practioner was so charmed by Miss Wilsie, she made house calls just to visit. Sometimes I took her on errands like the hairdresser, the supermarket and whatever, and we went out to concerts and movies once in a while, just to get out. I guess she was my best friend.

While I was rolling all this backstory around in my mind, Miss Wilsie was pondering my freelance job.

Finally, she said, "Well, someone needs to do this. It's very hard to deliver unpleasant news, and it can create a lot of bad feeling. But if you, a stranger, drop by and say something then they never see you again, I suppose that does take the sting out of things." She tapped a long red nail against her cheek. "The trouble is, some people want to kill the messenger. So you do have to be prepared to make a quick getaway."

"I hadn't thought about that, but that's true. I'll have to learn to think on my feet. And run faster."

"I can't think of anything worse

than telling someone their personal hygiene needs work, but you know, there's always someone out there who needs to pay more attention. There was a woman at the country club whose perfume could have choked a horse, for instance, back in the Fifties. We left a note on her locker while she was out on the links. Cowardly, but dear lord, she must have bathed in Shalimar." Miss Wilsie waved a hand in front of her face as if brushing away a foul odor.

As I was sitting there drinking Grey Goose, I thought about how I wanted to be just like Miss Wilsie when I grew up. Stinking rich, healthy and not giving a damn.

I opened my mouth to tell her about Susan, but then she hit me with the bomb.

"As a matter of fact, Mari, there's some bad news I would like you to deliver for me."

Uh oh. "What's that?" I asked. If she'd asked me to kill a dragon, I would have done it for her, especially after a couple of vodka and tonics.

"It's Freddie," she said flatly.

"Oh, jeebus, whatever does he want now?"

Miss Wilsie's lips tightened into a thin line. "He's on that thing about how I should go into a nursing home again. Assisted living, they call it now."

"Just tell him hell no, like you always do," I said.

"This time, he's getting a lawyer," Wilsie said ominously

.

Chapter Nine

"**W**hat does- - -" I started to say, but the door knocker sounded.

"That's him and Myrtle now," Wilsie said. "Be a dear and go answer it, please."

I opened the door a crack and sure enough, it was Frederick Wilson Sharpless and his lovely wife Myrtle.

We looked at each other with ill-concealed loathing.

"I've come to see Mother," Freddie said imperiously, and I reluctantly opened the door.

Freddie was older than me by several years, and I'd always disliked him, even when we were kids. He was creepy and sneaky and a bully tattletale, for starters. Age had not improved his looks. He was paunchy and balding with a mustache that did nothing for his unfortunate chin. His pale blue eyes gave him a weak look. He was greedy, shifty and totally for himself. My mother used to put it down to his being an only child, but I think he was just a born sneak. His latest venture, becoming an enthusiastic member of the Church of Angry Jesus, was inspired by being able to run things. Fred loved running things.

His lovely bride Myrtle was plump and obedient, dowdy in her shapeless clothes. She basically did whatever Freddie told her to do, which enraged me no end.

"Where's Mother?" Freddie asked, brushing right past me without as much as a hello. Myrtle sort of tried to smile weakly at me, but it never reached her eyes.

I followed them through the maze of heavy Baltimore furniture into the back room and stood protectively behind Miss Wilsie's recliner.

"Drinking, Mother?" Freddie said disapprovingly by way of greeting.

"Having a nice vodka and tonic," Miss Wilsie replied dryly. "I'd ask if you and Myrtle, hello, Myrtle dear, would join me, but I know your new church frowns on drinking, smoking, dancing or any other form of pleasure."

And that was the thing. Somewhere along the line, Freddie had discovered a wonderful outlet for his control freak personality in this small breakaway sect. As best I could figure, the religion he believed in thought everyone who wasn't in their tiny congregation was on the highway to hell, Route 666.

"And you, Mari. Have you found Jesus yet?" he asked me as he always did.

"I wasn't aware Jesus was lost," I replied as usual because I knew it drove him crazy. I had my own personal reasons for loathing Freddie and Myrtle, aside from their occasional forays into trying to bully Miss Wilsie into selling her house, her antiques and signing over all her money to Freddie, because she was getting too old to live alone. I was pretty sure that money would go right into his pocket, but he was Miss Wilsie's only offspring, so she loved him. I don't think she liked him much, but she loved him.

I trusted him about as far as I could throw him. He was truly a weasel and in a few paragraphs, I'll tell you why.

As a cradle Episcopalian, Miss Wilsie thought his new church was one step above snake handling. As a cradle Episcopalian, she believed in sermons and sinning quietly, with a martini afterward. She loathed the Church of Angry Jesus, not just for their belief everyone but them was going to hell, but for their, shall we say, fire and brimstone bigotry.

"Well, I suppose you're going to launch into one of your tedious prayers now, although I have told you many times that my soul doesn't need saving."

"Machiavelli said 'Heaven for the climate, but Hell for the company'," I quoted angelically. I'm such a bitch.

He didn't dare glare at his mother, but Freddie gave me a look that would peel my paint, if I had paint to peel. But I don't scare easily.

That was Fred's cue to launch into a long, rambling prayer full of poor syntax and questionable grammar from a man who'd been so expensively educated.

"Lord, thou knowest that I am a Christian, and spent my life doing for other people."

"Amen," Myrtle said.

He could believe that all he wanted, and so could the church he belonged to, but I knew he was cunning, dishonest and the kind of hypocrite who gives hypocrites a bad name. For all his conversion chatter, money was always his true god. "And we pray, dear Lord, for those who have fallen away, and women who have placed themselves above the men."

Out of respect for Miss Wilsie, I bit my tongue.

He really had to bring up

submissive women. Just had to dig in that knife. I wanted to punch him, the bigot.

Myrtle's chins shook. "Praise God!" she exclaimed. I wanted to slap her silly too. She was weak, but she could have stood up for Jamey. After all, he was her child, too. Her only child. Jamey, seeing which way the wind was blowing in a small town years ago, had disappeared and been long gone, much to Miss Wilsie's dismay.

Fred had taken a deep breath and was about to pray some more when Wilsie spoke up.

"Amen!" She said giving him the hairy eyeball.

"And we also pray for our elected officials, that they see the godly ways of - - -" Fred continued. He'd been trained as a lawyer, and he always talked as if he were summing up before a jury.

"I said, AMEN!" Wilsie repeated loudly, and even Fred got the hint.

Wilsie Sharpless was sharper than the whole pack of her relatives put together, and she didn't miss a trick, although they thought she did. This suited her just fine. How she ended up with such a dead end, humorless son, I don't know, but I suspect he took after her late husband. Allegedly, Freddie had a law practice, but I'd never heard that he practiced. There were rumors he'd stolen from an estate he was supposed to be handling, but they were just rumors, and the whole thing was hushed up.

"Now why did you want to see me, Freddie? You so rarely call unless you want something." She found Fred's religiosity tiresome, and his self-righteousness downright annoying. "The one person I miss the most is Jamey," Miss Wilsie added, just because she knew it annoyed him.

"Mom, Jamey has been dead to us for years," Fred reminded her, the way he always did when Miss Wilsie brought up her beloved grandson. From what I remembered, Jamey was a lot like Miss Wilsie and not a bit like Fred and Myrtle. "We cast out the sinning homosexual from our midst."

"You drove him away from here by making his life unbearable, and he cut us all out of his life. Even me. Do you think I'm ever going to forget that, Freddie? My grandson? Your son, who you should have loved and accepted."

"Don't let's think about unpleasant things today," Myrtle put in quickly, shifting her bulk into a seat.

"Jamey isn't an unpleasant subject to me. I just wish he hadn't cut off contact with me." Miss Wilsie was wistful. "I still miss him, all these years later. We used to laugh and have so much fun together..."

"We'd better be going soon," Fred cut in. "I've got to go a farm auction. They foreclosed on Levin Willis's property. Ought to be able to pick up a bargain or two."

"And I've got to get to WalMart," Myrtle said.

Fred pulled some papers from his jacket pocket. He cleared his throat, and for a minute I thought he was going to deliver another sermon. "Now, Mother, as you know, I worry about you alone in this house."

"I'm not alone. If I tap on the bedroom wall, Mari can hear me on the other side and come right over," Miss Wilsie pointed out. Vanessa comes in three or four times a week, and Katherine comes by and checks me out at least once a week. And I have my boring friends in the garden club and the DAR to amuse me. And I'm doing better than many 80-year-olds. I do yoga, I walk, I garden a little and I keep up with the world, which is more than I can say for you two. When was the last time you worked out?"

"Well, Mother, I think you'd be better off in assisted living. People would be around you all the time, and you wouldn't have to worry about this great big house or all these things, which are family things, after all. And I worry about you getting vague."

"She's about as vague as Stephan Hawking!" I put in angrily.

Freddie gave me a skim milk

smile. "I'm the head of the family now, and the Bible says the man is the head of the household and should be obeyed . . . "

"As the matriarch, my power trumps yours, in chess and in real life, Freddie. I gave you the farm and all the farm property when your father died, and together with your trusts, that certainly gives you enough money to live comfortably. You have a law degree, maybe you should get some clients. Or a degree in theology. This jumped-up church is just tacky. One of my friends actually asked me if you handled snakes out there!"

"It's not that I would want the house and the antiques for myself," Freddie whined. "But it really would help me rest if I knew you were taken care of. And you'd be made comfortable for the rest of your life at Shady Pines Manor."

"They'll carry me out of here feet first," Miss Wilsie sipped her vodka. "This is my house, I have my money and you're not getting your hands on either one."

Freddie shook his head in sorrow. "That's why I had Ray Welsh draw up this power of attorney. Mother, I'm sorry, but I think you're getting on in years and you're not yourself anymore. I need to look after your interests."

"Ray Welsh?" I exclaimed. "That sleazy courthouse barnacle? They came this close to disbarring him for fooling around with his female clients! I wouldn't let him defend me on a traffic ticket."

"Ray is a fine, Christian man," Myrtle offered tentatively, looking for approval to Fred, who nodded. "And it would be a conflict of interest for Freddie to handle your case, and Ray is a member of our church."

"I hate to do this, Mother, but I've prayed over it, and God told me it's for the best if I petition the court to allow me to take over your affairs. If you'll just sign this durable power of attorney. . ."

Wilsie pulled herself up out of

her chair and pointed one long red
fingernail at him. Talk about majestic
wrath. She might have been a Barbarian
queen sentencing a prisoner to death.
Years of doing exactly as she pleased
had honed her skills wonderfully. She
didn't even glance at the papers, which
were wilting in his hand.

"I'm giving you fifteen seconds
to get out of here and never come back
again. As far as I'm concerned, I have no
son. I spent my life handing you things
on a silver platter. In return, you drove
away my grandson and made my life a
misery with your canting, pious
hypocrisy and your sloth. Out! Both of
you! Out! And if I need to file a
restraining order on you, I'll do it. Try to
get Ray Welsh after me. I went to
dancing school with him. He was a
snake then and he's a snake now. And
there's certainly nothing wrong with my
mind, although I worry about yours."

Fred turned the color of a
poinsettia, and his face puffed out. I
really thought he was going to stroke out
there and then, but no such luck. Myrtle

rose and tried to clutch his arm, whimpering, but he pushed her away with a great deal of force. I rushed over to catch her, but Fred grabbed her arm and dragged her along with him to the front door.

"This isn't over yet!" he yelled. "I'm going to make sure I'm in charge! I'm going to get Ray to have you declared senile! You're going down, old lady!"

"Not if you go down first!" I yelled. "I know every lawyer and every judge in the tri-county area. You try to touch her and you're dead meat!"

"That's assault! That's assault!" Fred screamed.

"It's not assault. It's a terroristic threat, siccing one lawyer on another," I corrected him. "The door is that way."

After I made sure they were out of the house, I went back to Miss Wilsie, who was a little shaken but fixing herself another vodka.

"Well," she said in a shaky voice. "That went well, didn't it?"

I decided it wasn't a great time to tell her about Susan being temporarily camped out with me.

Chapter Ten

When I went upstairs, I found Susan packing her few things into her duffel bag. "Marianna, you're not going to believe what happened! I've got a job boat sitting a billionaire's yacht! He's going to be in China for months, and he needs someone to take care of his boat while he's gone! I'll be living aboard her down at the Boatworks! Rent free! In fact, he's paying me! All I have to do is routine maintenance, and I can walk about thirty feet to work! I'm leaving right now. I can't wait to get started!"

She was so excited she hugged me. I was so relieved and happy she was finally getting a break that I hugged her back.

"Come have lunch in a couple of days after I settle in," she asked me.

"I'd like that." I bid her farewell

at the door and breathed a sigh of relief.
I'd had enough drama for one day.

**

A lot of times, people who own
expensive boats they only use once or
twice a year will hire someone to look
after their investment when she's tied up
in a marina or a boatyard. Like a house
that's not lived in, an empty boat can fall
prey to all kinds of neglect. If there's a
boat bum, as they call them, aboard to
keep up routine maintenance and so
forth, it's a good thing. And sometimes
the boat bum gets to go on trips to the
islands in winter and the Maine coast in
summer in exchange for helping with the
navigation and the chores. Best of all,
they get a modest salary and a free crash
pad. It was a deal I wish I could have
lucked into, but I'm mechanically
incompetent and I get seasick on blue
water. And I don't take orders well.

So, there I was at Saturday
lunchtime, feeling a little peckish,
strolling around among the hulls up on
the stands, the travel lift, the boatyard
smells of urethane, fiberglass and freshly

cut wood, looking for slip 3C among the hulls and spires along the narrow catwalks. The tide was high, and it slapped gently against the pilings, one of those rare nice summer days when the sky is full of puffy clouds and there's no stinking thick humidity or heat.

I found Slip 3C. I was looking for some kind of houseboat or a cabin cruiser or a nice schooner, maybe. Something modestly immodest. What I found, at the end of the dock, in deep water, was a hull that would have made Moby Dick think he'd found his true love.

I looked over, then I looked up and up some more. *Miss Mindie* said the name on the trailboard. At least Moby's girlfriend had a name. The boat was huge, a fiberglass tub you might expect to see at Cannes or Exuma with some starlet in a bikini lounging on the afterdeck. The hull must draw about six or seven feet, I guessed, and at low tide, would rest on the bottom.

Hailing it from the dock would have been useless. If Susan were aboard, she wouldn't be able to hear me. There was a gangplank leading to the main deck, so I climbed up the ramp. When I got to the bulkheads, I called "Ahoy! Permission to board!" as if I'd had some home training. "It's Marianna! Susan!"

In a few seconds, a sliding glass door opened and my Alaskan waif grinned, beckoning me in. "Hey!" She grinned. "Wait until you see this!"

I stepped into the main cabin. It was bigger than my entire apartment, teak stippled with a faux finish. All the furniture and lighting was bolted down, as you might expect from an ocean-going vessel, but there was nothing uncomfortable or cramped about this room. Big comfy chairs, cocktail tables, all kinds of rich people nautical bric a brac.

The place was done in a kind of gilt and Caribbean blue, and before I could inhale the essence of a lot of much money and a professional interior designer, we passed on through a smaller dining room-bar area and down a hatchway into a galley that would have passed muster with Martha Stewart. Beyond that was the for'casle. with three whole cabins for the crew. You could have bivouacked the entire Maryland National Guard in there.

"This is where I'm sleeping," Susan indicated the largest crew cabin with a double berth, portholes and, she was pleased to show me, a good sized head with a walk-in shower, an enclosed head and a large sink and counter.

"This is the crew's quarters? It's bigger and nicer than my bedroom in the apartment," I teased. "Girl, you landed in some high corn."

Susan spun around the room. "If that means I came out of this good, I sure did. The owner said I could use one of the staterooms, but this suits me fine. It's got all the hot water and modern plumbing you could ask for!" Impulsively, she hugged me. "And I have you to thank for it. If you hadn't made me come clean," she giggled, "I'd probably be jobless. But I told Finn the whole story, and he called the guy who owns this boat who was looking for a boat bum sitter, and, well here I am."

I felt pretty good about myself, I must say. It's not that often that I don't screw something up one way or the other.

Susan got us some fancy craft beer I'd never even heard of, then we toured the staterooms, the media room, the navigation room and a bunch of other stuff. The master suite stateroom even had a saltwater aquarium, which a man came and looked at once a week, she told me. He also checked the engine room and other exotic stuff. Maybe it was sour grapes, but it occurred to me this tub was decorated like an expensive Las Vegas suite, some decorator's idea of a nautical theme. The worst taste money could buy. For some reason this cheered me up enormously in my poverty.

When we got back to the kitchen, the oven timer went off, and I settled down at the bar to eat tortellini salad and tomato caprese. It had been a long time since I'd had a home-cooked meal. Evidently, gourmet cooking was among

Susan's many skills.

"...So, here I am, and for the first time in a long time, I feel safe," Susan was telling me. "Clean, safe and sheltered. You have no idea how long it's been, and how grateful I am to you for making all this happen. Back in Alaska, things were pretty rough, even when they were good. I grew up way out, and then when my parents died, we were shifted around among foster families."

Just as we were about to dig in, and settle down for some girl talk, Finn walked in.

"Am I late?" he asked, making himself at home on the stool next to Susan, and helping himself to lunch. The way he smiled at her made me wonder if they were more than just employer-employee.

If I was disappointed, I really had no right to be, I reminded myself. These two had a lot in common, like boats. They worked together. All I'd done was clean up Susan's act a little. Always a fairy godmother, never a god.

Chapter Eleven

It just seemed like it happened one day. Spring turned into summer, and summer heated up until it was so humid the atmosphere was like breathing Raspberry Jell-O. We didn't hear anything more from Fred. "My son's always been all hat and no cattle," Miss Wilsie told me as we sipped our drinks on the front porch one evening, watching the world go by.

"You still need to lawyer up," I said darkly. "Get your own lawyer."

"I'll get around to it," Miss Wilsie promised, then told me some juicy gossip about the personal life of the most judgmental dowager of the local DAR chapter.

So I put it out of my mind, which was stupid.

***

Good citizen that I am, I continued to look for real employment, but nothing appeared, even as my unemployment was about to run out. But the bad news business had begun to take off, purely by word of mouth.

At first, I didn't take it seriously. My next call came a couple of weeks after the Betty Breakup and the Case of the Bad BO, and I thought it was a joke.

"I'm a friend of Betty's, and she told me you tell people off," said matter-of-fact voice one morning into my phone.

"That's right," I replied, stifling a yawn. It was eleven o'clock and I was still asleep. Unemployment does that to me.

"Well, this is Sylvia, and we got a clacking gum chewer that is driving the whole office crazy. Even the boss don't want to tell him to lay it off, because he's sensitive. Ernie, the gum clacker, not the boss. Our boss only cares about the sales we make. We're a marketing company."

I reached for a pen and a piece of paper. "I can handle that. What's the address?"

Thus armed, I went to Jump and Buckett Marketing Solutions back in the office park out behind the WalMart. Who doesn't want to make a telemarketer's life miserable? Revenge, I gloated, was mine.

Sylvia, a middle-aged woman with an enormous bouffant, greeted me in the reception area. She never even cracked a smile as she looked me up and down as if she doubted I was up to the job. "I hope you can talk to him," she told me without preamble. "He's driving us all nuts. All day long with the clack clack clack clack." She used a pen to point me into the small cubicle farm, where I followed the loud clacking to the carrel of the culprit, a middle-aged, balding man with a bow tie and the look of a scared rabbit. The tight, windowless space made me instantly claustrophobic. I couldn't imagine what it was like to work in an environment like this. It had to be bad, all this and people swearing at

you and hanging up the phone. Just as he
had to be named Ernie, as if he'd been
condemned from birth to be an invisible
cubicle man.

No even one looked at me as I
marched down the aisle between the
rows of workers. But I knew by instinct
they all were in on it, and knew who I
was and why I was here, mostly because
no one would make eye contact.
Suddenly their computers and their
posters of cute kittens and sailboats were
more interesting than the messenger in
their midst. I even noted the Big Boss
hovering in the doorway of his office,
waiting for the show.

I felt like a process server or a
repo man or someone even more
unwelcome among civilized people.

Other than the clacking, he
looked pretty normal. A jowly middle-
aged Ernie in a short sleeved shirt
working away at a computer. Clack,
clack, clack, headset perched on his bald
head. The smell of minty mint hovered
powerfully in the air, and he sounded
like a rhythm band. I could see where

this would really get under your skin if you had to hear it all day and be yelled at by perfect strangers.

I leaned over and said "Ernie."

He looked up expectantly, shifting the wad of gum from one jowl to the other.

I smiled at him. "I'm sorry to have to tell you this, but I've been hired by your colleagues to make a suggestion."

His smile wavered. I felt bad, but I pushed on.

"Uh, it's your gum."

He looked really relieved. All the muscles in his smile collapsed.

"I thought maybe you were going to tell me I was fired. There've been rumors I'm not makin' the sales. . ."

"No, it's the way you chew gum. No one cares if you chew gum, but the clacking is driving everyone nuts."

He frowned. "I clack my gum?" He really didn't know, even as he gave a loud crack.

I nodded. "Pretty loudly, too. You've really got snapping that gum down to a fine art. Too bad they don't have contests for gum clacking, because you could win."

He shook his head, puzzled. "I had no idea I was doing it." He shifted the wad in his mouth. "I'm trying to stop smoking. What's wrong with that? Gum helps me!"

"That's the way it is. You do something, it's a habit and you don't even realize you're doing it. But your colleagues do, and while everyone here really, really likes you, they wish you'd stop doing it. It's making them crazy." I had no idea if they liked him or not, but it doesn't hurt to stoke it on when you're kind of insulting people.

"Like Debbie's humming?" he asked a little too loudly, and I realized I'd pushed a button. "At least I'm trying to smoke smoking. That's what the gum is for, so I can stop smoking. I don't know why Debbie hums all that Nickelback all day. I hate Nickelback. Everyone hates Nickelback."

Everyone, including me, turned to look at Debbie, who was about twenty with a pierced nose, eyebrow and lip. Debbie, in turn, looked around the office and found no sympathy.

"I like Nickelback," she exclaimed defensively, eyes darting around the room.

"Nickelback is still a thing?" I asked.

"Well, no one likes to hear you hum all day long," Ernie said. "You've got a hum that could cut steel. As long as I keep clacking my gum, I don't have to listen to you humming!"

Debbie blinked. "Well, I never!" she said, opening and closing her mouth, the stud in her tongue clicking against her teeth. I wondered if she kept away from magnets with all that metal attached to her face. "At least Nickelback doesn't smell as bad as that stale perfume Susie wears. You could gag a maggot with that shit. And you come home and you can't get that sweet, stinky smell out of your clothes."

From somewhere behind me, I heard a gasp and some choked laughter. Clearly, office politics were getting toxic and long suppressed grudges were coming to the surface. And here I'd thought the smell in the air was cheap room deodorizer, it was strong, it was sweet, and it had that cardboard smell stale perfume can get.

"It's all that Barry Manilow," someone said.

A middle aged woman with glasses flushed up to the roots of her hair. I felt bad for her. Humiliating times in the cubical farm.

"I like Jungle Gardenia," she said, blinking back tears. Ever since my stroke, I don't smell things the way I used to. Why didn't someone take me aside and tell me nicely?"

Because, it struck me, people are basically cowards who can't tell each other the truth because they're afraid people won't like them. And we all want to be liked. And because we want to be liked, I have a job, because I didn't have a stake in this.

"And since we're on the subject, I'm sick of sitting in the break room listening to Debbie chattering on and on to Sylvia, gossiping everyone's business and tearing everyone's character to shreds. . ."

"Well, you never hesitate to put in your opinion," Sylvia snapped.

And the place erupted into a brawl as long nurtured, poisonously repressed grudges suddenly exploded. I stood there, gobsmacked, as the insults and rage echoed through the room. If there was anyone on any of those lines listening, they must have thought the place was caught in a tornado.

"There's just one thing I don't get," Ernie said to me as we walked to the door, everyone ignoring us while they tore into each other. "Why didn't someone say something to me? Why go through a stranger?"

I shook my head. He was a perfectly nice man, with a photo of a nice family on his desk. "I guess no one wanted to break the bad news. That seems to be what I do. Deliver bad news to people."

On my way out, I pulled my check out of Sylvia's fingers before she even noticed. She was telling a man with a crew cut that she was sick and tired of his dirty jokes.

The supervisor was standing in the door of his office, watching the melee. "I don't suppose," I said to him as I passed, "That you'd have a job opening for me?"

I didn't even wait for his reply. At least I could say I applied for a job here and be telling the truth to Unemployment.

Chapter Twelve

Fresh off my last success, I took another job delivering bad news, the kind no one wants to hear. It paid well and I was on a roll. And I was ready for any reaction I got, even one that might break my heart.

I met the guy in the park at the arranged time. He was probably in his thirties, not handsome, but pleasant, with a slightly buck toothed smile. He took the forms from me and scanned them, frowning, then handed them back to me as if they burned his fingers. "Does this mean Brooke's not my daughter?" he asked.

"The DNA test says no. Danny's her biological father. I'm sorry she didn't have the courage to tell you this herself." I took a deep breath. "I think she's ashamed."

For a minute, I thought he was

going to kill the messenger. His fists rolled up and his face darkened. I took a step back. No wonder she was afraid to tell him, I thought. He's got a temper. I took another step back, ready to run.

But instead of hitting me, he straightened up and put his shoulders back, held his head up. "A piece of paper don't mean nothing," he told me. "Brooke's been my daughter since the day she was born, and she'll always be my daughter. I love that little girl more than life itself."

He looked over my shoulder, at the swings, where a woman was pushing a little ginger-haired girl, but watching him. "Brooke's mine, and that's that. Any fool can be a sperm donor, but it takes a man to be a father. And I'm her daddy."

"You tell her that," I said.

"I mean to. And you can give her back them papers. They don't make no nevermind to me. Brooke's my kid, and that's that."

I watched as he strode across the field toward the swings, his arms opened wide.

Sometimes, the good overrules the bad.

***

It wasn't just the Wednesday meetings of the Santimoke Gazette that made me happy. We continued up online, and once local businesses realized we had eyeballs on the copy, they started buying more advertising. It wasn't much, but it kept us in beer and cheeseburgers. I covered my share of stories, went out crabbing with the watermen, attended the Jaycees chicken barbecue to hear the local politicians natter on, drowsed through my fair share of town and county government meetings.

When our meeting was over, I'd find Finn sitting at the bar after choir practice. We seemed to cross paths here, something else I could look forward to on Wednesdays. I'd sit at the bar with him, feeling my attraction to him bubbling. I was trying to hide it though, since I had a feeling his thing was for

Susan. So, I'd slide onto the bar stool next to him and grin like we were buddies and I didn't think he was the hottest thing in town.

"How's Susan doing?" I asked.

"Well, she doesn't smell," Finn grinned. "She's something special, you know? She can do just about anything." He'd shake his head in admiration.

At first, I had tried to swallow that little knot of jealousy in the back of my mind. Of course, he'd be impressed by one of those strong capable women like Susan, competent outdoorsy girls who could heft a fifty-pound sack of cement. As far as the outdoors was concerned, I was just as happy to lie by the pool.

"So, how's the bad news business?" he finally asked me, grinning as if it were all a joke. "I see you're still in one piece, so no one's killed the messenger yet, huh?"

Those green eyes teased me. I got defensive. "It's something to make money doing. And it affects people's lives, you know. I'm providing a service, Finn."

I don't know why I was so defensive about it. "It isn't rocket science. It isn't a cure for cancer. It isn't world peace, although maybe if they used someone like me to tell the truth to power, it could lead to world peace." I sounded sullen, and I hated myself for it. I also hated that he thought it was such a huge joke. But he wasn't getting the checks. "I realize a guy who babysits wooden boats for rich people might not see it as a viable job, but it's working so far."

Finn gave me a serious look. " I just worry one of these days you're gonna give somebody some bad news and they're gonna hurt the messenger."

"I'm a big girl. I can take care of myself," I replied.

What could possibly go wrong?

I was careful to keep it light with him, even though there was a lonely, celibate part of me that wanted to rise off the barstool and tear his t-shirt off to get at those abs and pecs and biceps. And that night, I had my chance.

I was telling him about the shootout at the telemarketers. "And then, the girl with all the piercings says..."

"Last call!" The bartender yelled at that very minute. Finn looked down regretfully at his empty Corona.

"I've got some beer back at my place," I managed to say. "I just live about a block away on Water Street. Want to come over?"

Finn nodded. "I thought you'd never ask," he said and my heart did a double dutch. "Let's go."

So, we went.

"We don't want to wake up Miss Wilsie," I was saying as I let us in my back door. So far, Finn had been a perfect gentleman, but I was hoping when we got upstairs that would change.

"What's that noise?" he asked, standing in the door, his head cocked to one side.

Ever so faintly, I heard a voice

coming from the main house. "Marianna? Is that you?"

I tore through the connecting door. "Miss Wilsie?" I called. Finn was right behind me.

She was lying in a heap on the kitchen floor, her robe spread out around her. Blood was streaming down her face from her forehead. "Oh, I thought you'd never get here," she said faintly. "I got up on the stool to get something out of the high kitchen cabinet and I lost my balance. . ." She blinked at Finn. "Oh, helloooo," she whispered, always the belle.

I grabbed some paper towels to staunch the blood. She was as pale as death and shaky.

"Head wounds are more blood than trauma, but you can't be certain she didn't break something on the way down," Finn was saying as he ran his fingers over her arms and legs. "Can you hear me, ma'm? Do you feel any pain?"

"If you'd just use that cell phone I gave you," I fussed because I was frightened and upset. I'd stanched the blood on her forehead, but the cut was pretty deep.

"Those things give you cancer, I told you," Miss Wilsie grunted. "Ouch!"

"I'm calling the paramedics," Finn said. "She might have broken something. Don't try to move her. Let them do it." He already had his cell phone out. "I won't let it give me cancer," he told Miss Wilsie who managed a smile for a good looking guy.

She pressed her hand into his. "Aren't you a handsome one?" she asked. "I'll be fine, if I can just get up- - - oh!" She collapsed back against the linoleum in pain. And she didn't argue with Finn anymore.

After the paramedics arrived, I sent Finn on home. It didn't look as if we were going to have a nightcap after all, and there wasn't much he could do, haunting the hospital with a work day ahead of him. As I waited and waited, missed chances weren't the first thing on my mind, but I'd have to admit they flickered across my consciousness.

After what seemed like an eternity of waiting, I finally went up to the nurses' station and asked about Miss Wilsie. The nurse on shift gave me an exhausted look. "I can't tell you anything. You're not family. Her family's with her. You may as well go home. We're keeping her overnight."

It was on the tip of my tongue to give this unpleasant woman some news she didn't want to hear, but I was helpless. They'd called Miss Wilsie's next of kin, the lovely and talented Fred, and I was off the loop.

"If it's any consolation," the nurse added with a sour smile, "She's in there giving her son holy hell. You may as well go home. We're taking her upstairs as soon as they scan her for broken bones. You can come by tomorrow."

Feeling chastened and tired, I went home so late it was almost morning. I was about to head directly upstairs when I heard a strange noise coming from Miss Wilsie's side of the door.

Maybe she'd left the TV on when she
went to the hospital, although I didn't
remember it.

With a sigh, I unlocked the
connecting door and walked right in on a
stranger.

Chapter Thirteen

I've never fainted in my life, but I've got to say, standing there in the semi-darkness, looking at the dark silhouette of an intruder was the best opportunity ever.

Instead, I gasped, "You better get out now." My voice sounded uncertain and squeaky, even to me. I wished I had my .38, but it was upstairs in the back of my winter clothes closet with a lock on it. A broom handle was good enough.

"Marianna! It's me! Jamey Sharpless!"

He moved into the light, and I could see he had long hair and a pair of chandelier earrings. I flipped the wall switch with my elbow. Light flooded the room, blinding us both, but nobody moved. It took me a couple of seconds to figure out what was wrong with this picture.

"You're not Jamey. Jamey is a man. You're a woman!" Score one for me. He, I mean she, was a woman. A tall, big- boned woman, but a woman nonetheless. A woman with beautifully highlighted, well cut blonde hair, a terrific magenta sheath and some gold jewelry I would have killed for. I did wonder where she found a pair of designer shoes in that size, but the pieces still weren't falling together.

"I'm Jamey Sharpless. Where's Grammy? I've been waiting for her."

"You're Miss Wilsie's grandson! You're supposed to be dead or disappeared! You've got a hell of a nerve showing up here after all these years." She did look like I remembered Jamey from decades ago. Except, of course, he was a she, which was confusing me on top of everything else. But as you've seen, I'm easily confused.

Jamey threw up her hands. "It's time to stop living a lie. Grammy's going to be 90 soon. I want to see her before she dies. That is if the sight of me as a woman doesn't kill her first. And I don't care what Dad says anymore. I might be dead to my parents, but I want to see Grammy!"

I turned off my phone, propped the broom against the wall and sank into one of Miss Wilsie's Baltimore chairs. "Your grandmother took a little fall tonight. She's spending the night at the hospital, just so they can keep an eye on her." I held up my hand. "It's nothing serious. I don't think she broke anything. In fact, she's in great shape for a woman her age. Still drives, still gets around, interested in everything. But this---you--- is gonna rock her world."

"Are you sure she's okay? I want to see her, but not if she's in the hospital. I've come all this way, and it took me a lot of courage and therapy to get back here to this ---armpit."

I assured him Miss Wilsie was just fine, and in fact better than people half her age. "I'm sorry. This is just, that is, I'm gobsmacked. Jamey? Is that really you? I'm gonna need to absorb this."

"Well, of course you are," Jamey

said. She sat down on the couch, crossing her legs. "And you can just imagine how I feel. I'm so sorry. I knew this would be difficult, but. . . Let me start at the beginning. . . "

***

"Scrapple!" Jamey exclaimed. "I haven't had scrapple since, well, since I left the Shore."

I flipped the meat over in the skillet. "I haven't had breakfast at three a.m. in years. You want your eggs sunny side up or scrambled?"

We were in my little kitchen. Jamey was monitoring the bagels in the toaster oven and I was tending to the scrapple, trying to get that nice, thin crisp crust he remembered from his childhood.

Jamey poured me another mimosa. "I'll do the eggs. I make a very nice omelet. I took a cordon bleu cooking course when I was transitioning. It was a part of liberating myself."

"I'm getting a real education here," I sipped my mimosa. "Leading the sheltered life on the Eastern Shore, I haven't met a whole lot of post-operative transsexuals." I sort of slurred it. You try saying "Post-operative transsexuals" with half a bottle of Prosecco inside you. "I mean, I used to know a couple of drag queens, but it was more of a performance thing, y'know? One did Cher and one did Jackie O."

Jamey shrugged. "Show business. A completely different thing from transitioning into a woman. It's rough, feeling all your life that you've been born in the wrong body. And then trying to prove you're a manly man by joining the military."

"Well, you proved you were brave," I pointed out. "I wouldn't have had the balls, excuse me, to go into combat. Or maybe I would have. I dunno."

"Brave has nothing to do with gender identification," Jamey shrugged. " 'Lately it occurs to me, what a long strange trip it's been'," he quoted that old chestnut from the Dead.

He had had quite a long, strange trip.

"Talk about confused. At first I thought I was gay. When I got out of the military, I headed for San Francisco. Did the whole gay scene. The drag and everything. Long story short, eventually I met a couple of guys who'd actually had the surgery. It's a whole psychological process. You live like a woman. You start taking hormones; you're in therapy, individual and group. They really want you to be sure you're born into the wrong gender. Now, I run what you might call a school or workshops for people who are transitioning to female. How to use makeup without looking like a clown. How to dress for your new body. Style. Some of these people have no idea how to style themselves and you have to start at square one. How to walk and use your female body. How to express your true self. It's much more complex than that, but you get the general idea. Sort of like a finishing school. It's not for everyone, and some people think we're just awful, but we do well enough to make a decent living, and we provide a service for those who want it. If it's not for you, that's fine. Let me top that off for you, Marianna."

"Yeah, I think I need a little buzz for this one. Not because of you, but because this is the last thing I was expecting when I came home tonight. Jeeze, what a story this would make!"

He, I mean she, held up a large, beautifully manicured hand with a gold and emerald ring I would have killed for. "No. No story. I don't even want anyone to know I'm back here. And in a way, it's because of you."

I flipped the scrapple. It sizzled nicely in the pan, wafting the aroma of pork, sage and pepper. "Me? Now I'm even more confused. "Miss Wilsie thinks you left here for good. That's what Fred and Myrt said."

She sat up straight and threw one shapely leg over the other. "To all intents and purposes, I'm dead. Do you know how much paperwork it's taken over the years to change my gender on all of my ID? And of course, my father pretends I'm dead so he can spare himself the disgrace of having a son like me. I would have stayed in Marin County and my new life if I hadn't happened to stumble on that article you wrote in that online newspaper about Grammy's 89th birthday. As much as I hated this place when I was growing up here, I keep up with the news from home. I almost thought Grammy was dead. Who knew she'd live to be 89?"

"Miss Wilsie is one strong lady. And when she finds out her favorite grandson, I mean, granddaughter is alive and well, she'll live another ten years plus! You have no idea how much she's missed you all these years. It broke her heart when you cut off contact."

"Dad said if she found out about me, it would kill her. Just kill her. I underestimated her." Jamey shook her head. "All these wasted years!"

I gulped my mimosa, spatula'd the scrapple on to a brown paper bag to drain off the grease and turned the flame on the burner down. "Jamey, you don't know your grandmother. She's one of the most open-minded, socially liberal people I've ever met in my life. She's not a wormy bigot like Fred. I mean, well he is your father, but he's a hypocrite and a creep and a crook and all kinds of stuff. If Miss Wilsie knew you were here and you didn't see her. . . it would kill her."

Jamey broke eggs into a bowl, briskly whipping them with a whisk. "I can't. I just can't. I want to see her, but I don't want to shock her. Now that I'm here, I'm not so sure this was a good idea. I should just catch the next plane to California."

I took a deep breath. Jamey smelled faintly of a vanilla musk rose scent, not at all unpleasant. In spite of myself, I grinned. She was more girl than I'd ever be.

I snapped to. "Your grandmother has told me a time or two that she's ready to go whenever the Lord decides to take her. She's 89, Jamey. That's a long time. She's old, she's tired, she's lived a life. And in spite of all that, she is one of the most delightful people I know. Everyone adores her. The old guys are crazy about her. The young guys are crazy about her. The one thing that she needs before she dies is to see you. I don't think she'd much care if you were a man, a woman or a vampire, as long as it was you. When you're her age, you've seen it all, and nothing surprises you. Now that you've come all the way back east, you owe it to her to see her and tell her who you are. And that you are alive and well. "

"But Dad- - - "

"Screw Fred," I said. "I'm sick of the Freds of this world and their bigotry and lies and greed. All Fred cares about is inheriting his mother's money. You wanna see your grandmother? I'm gonna make it happen. I owe it to her." I looked at Jamey thoughtfully. "You know, both your grandmother and I have a lot to learn about the transsexual experience. It's new to us. You're gonna have a lot of explaining to do for us."

"It's what I do," Jamey said gravely.

Chapter Fourteen

The next morning, we waited until about ten. By that time. Miss Wilsie would have been up for a while, had her breakfast, had her doctor come by, her vitals checked. Now she'd be watching whatever reality show Bravo was showing, the battling housewives or whatever other trash was on.

She was lying comfortably on the bed, propped up by a meadow of pillows, shaking her head at the high-heeled goings on. From time to time, she glanced down at the daily crossword in the *Washington Post*. The only sign she'd been in trouble was a bandage on her forehead. Otherwise, she looked none the worse for wear.

When she saw me peering in the door, her thoughtful expression turned into a welcoming smile. "Why,

Marianna! I was just thinking about you. As soon as the doctor signs the releases, I'm going home. Nothing broken, just a spill. What's six letter for 'long'?"

I came into the room and closed the door, taking a deep breath. "Miss Wilsie, I have a surprise for you, and I need to warn you it's going to be huge. Ginormous. Someone you never thought you'd see again is outside." As I spoke, I brushed out her hair.

"Who in the world? Oh, this is exciting! Is it my cousin Alice from Salisbury?" She beamed.

I washed her face and even put on a little makeup. She kept up a steady stream of chatter, asking me all kinds of questions.

"I can't wait to get out of here. I've got bridge club tomorrow. What's the surprise?

"I can't tell you. You'll see. I just want you to promise me you'll be calm, because this is going to be a surprise in more than one way."

When I had her fixed up to my

satisfaction, I opened the door. Excitement made her cheeks glow and her eyes sparkle. There was so little out of the ordinary in her days that it didn't take a lot to get her interested. I took a deep breath and beckoned. Dear lord, I thought, please don't let me be the cause of her having a heart attack.

Jamey stepped into the room.

"Grammy?" he asked.

It took her about two seconds to recognize him.

I told you she was sharp.

She opened her arms. "Jamey! Is that you?" she asked. "I knew you'd come back. Quick, Marianna, tell me I'm not dying and he's not coming to take me away."

"No, Grammy. I'm not dead and neither are you," Jamey said, striding across the room and embracing Miss Wilsie so tightly I thought he might break her. Gotta get my pronouns right, I remembered. She. S-h-e.

"Oh, Jamey! Let me look at you!

Well, it's nice to see you came out of the closet, or whatever they're calling it these days. Oh, they told me you'd cut us off! All these years!" They were both tearing up, beyond speech.

I had to leave the room. There must have been some dust or pollen or something in the air because my eyes were watering something fierce. When I stuck my head back in the door, Miss Wilsie said, "Come on, Marianna, help me get into my clothes. We've got to get out of here and get home before Fred shows up to hector me."

"This is the last place I want to see my parents," Jamey rolled his eyes. "We're sneaking out against medical advice. Grammy's fine. She just wants to avoid my father, and so do I."

I looked at my watch and realized I had a date with someone else's destiny today, so I needed to get moving, too.

***

An hour later, I pulled up in front of The Watertown School. It was a private day school, the kind of place you send your kids when you don't want them mixing with the commoners at the public high school. If you had money, this was where your kids went. I wasn't too fond of the place myself, having briefly attended there before being asked to leave and go to public school because of my grades and my attitude.

I sighed as I parked my car, got my visitor's badge from the front office, where Mrs. Krozinksi still recognized and disliked me after all these years.

"You poor thing," she said with surprising sympathy. "They're in the gym. Ms. Reynolds is expecting you. Mrs. Crawley isn't."

"Thanks for the heads up." I headed down the hallway, full of the rush of a familiar smell of adolescent, cafeteria food and disinfectant. Not much had changed since I'd roamed these halls, sneaking outside for a cigarette, dreading algebra class, avoiding the pack of mean girls and the bullying jocks as best I could.

The gym had had a couple of coats of fresh paint since I was last here, and a new set of bleachers. Otherwise, it still smelled of rank gym clothes, sweat and basketballs. There was a group of young girls in leotards working on a balance beam and a mat. Just the sight of them brought back memories of a sadist teaching gymnastics and a sick sense of failure.

The woman who was coaching this generation of gymnasts actually looked pretty nice, unlike the gorgon I'd had. She was demonstrating a forward roll when I came in, so I had a chance to check out the moms sitting on the bleachers. One of them wasn't sitting quietly like the rest. She was standing at the edge of the mat, screeching at a beleaguered little girl in a green leotard.

"Tuck and roll, Sydney, tuck and roll!" The woman, thin and taut with a strained, puckered expression, shouted and waved her arms in the air. "I keep telling you to tuck and roll!"

"Off the mat, please, Mrs. Crawley," the coach called wearily.

"You're not giving Sydney enough attention!" Mrs. Crawley trilled.

I swear, if she were any thinner, she could get a job as whip.

The coach finally saw me, and her shoulders sagged. "Take five!" she called to the girls as she came toward me.

"Thank you for doing this. "Mr. Crawley said this would be better than the police. He's a legacy and we want to help, but we have to be careful."

We both looked at Mrs. Crawley. Her unhappiness was almost palpable as she lectured the girl in the green leotard. The girl was a little chubby for gymnastics, more of a sign she was going into puberty than actual fat. And the kid looked miserable.

"Well, no time like the present," I said, sucking in my breath and walking across the gym floor toward Mrs. Crawley.

"I don't know what's wrong with you," she was telling her daughter, "If you'd just try a little harder, you could try out for the state team. . ."

The kid hung her head as if she'd been struck.

"Mrs. Crawley? Mrs. Angela Crawley?" I asked as I approached her.

She broke off, mid-rant and looked at me as if I was something she'd found on the bottom of her shoe.

I pulled the papers out of my pocketbook. "Court order, Mrs. Crawley. Dr. Crawley has been granted full custody of Sydney. You can leave now, and the doctor can pick her up as soon as you're off the premises."

I never saw anyone's face twist into such a mask of rage before. With a howl, she reached out for me with hands turned into claws and raked my face. I ducked just in time, but she landed me a pretty good blow on the side of my head anyway, howling like an animal.

This bitch ain't right, was what I was thinking as my head jerked back and she threw herself on me. I regained my balance just in time and grabbed her arms before she could hit me again.

Fortunately, the coach moved fast, and quickly had the woman's arms pinned behind her back. In the end, the school ended up calling the police, which they'd tried to avoid, since after all, this was an upscale private school, where these things didn't happen.

I was still rubbing my face and watching two uniformed officers and the boys' wrestling coach take her away, hopefully to get the help she obviously needed.

I was wondering what judge would have let that crazy lady have unsupervised custody in the first place when I saw Sydney sitting on the balance beam, looking as if someone had knocked the wind out of her.

All the other mothers had gathered up their girls and left, no doubt to spread the story of Mrs. Crawley's coo coo craziness all over the country club and the aerobics class.

I sat down beside Sydney. "Your dad's outside," I told her. "I'm sorry. I'm so sorry."

She looked at me. "Does this mean I won't have to take gymnastics anymore?" she asked.

Chapter Fifteen

The first thing in the morning, I had another job, so I didn't get to check into the events in Miss Wilsie's. Besides, I didn't want her to see the giant bruise on the side of my head and worry about me.

And after what happened, I was beginning to think I should charge combat pay.

I ran some errands and then stopped by the Beautiful Black Bombshell hair salon. Someone in Finn's church had hired me to tell a hairdresser she had bad breath, give her a new toothbrush, toothpaste, some Altoids and the name of a dentist in Chestertown who specialized in halitosis. Easy enough, right?

I should have known I was in trouble when I saw the size of her and her Resting Bitch Face expression. Some people have a natural sour expression, but she could stop a clock with that glower. And she towered over me, built like a wrestler. She looked at the offerings in my hand and my bright, friendly, phony smile. A smile that was wavering fast.

"What the hell is this?" she snarled. "Who the hell are you?" And yes, she had dragon breath that could melt plastic. Rotting meat topped with a thousand stale cigarettes. Sauron in all his glory couldn't have topped that halitosis.

"I've been asked by your partners to help you with your, uh, problem with oral hygiene." I was shrinking away. I don't scare easily, but she was big and butch and had fists like hams.

"Is this some kinda joke? Them damn bitches think they're so smart." She looked over my shoulder at two hairdressers deeply involved with their clients. "You think this is funny, Tiffany, Tanika? Huh? You think this is funny? You stinkin' damn ho', get outta my sight!"

With that, she took those big hands and shoved me by the shoulders. I fell back, stumbling into a station. Brushes, products and a client in aluminum foil wraps went flying. "I'll show you who's got bad breath, you stupid heifer!"

Between her breath and the push, I was gasping.

"Ronni, calm down!" A tiny lady, who looked as if Ronni could crush her with a finger, came flying out of the back and jumped on the bigger woman's shoulders. "Down! Calm down! If you don't calm down, you'll never braid hair in Watertown again!" The little woman hung on to the larger one like a dog on a bull. "This is why I wanted you to tell her," the little woman said to me as Ronni tried to buck her off. "I figured she wouldn't go off on you, a stranger and all! Ronni, stop it now! I mean it! Stop it or it's back to anger management for you."

And believe it or not, that little woman calmed that giantess down.

Ronni slumped and hung her head. "I'm sorry," she mumbled to me, the fight drained out of her, "I don't handle criticism well."

"Your check's at the front desk, under the paperweight," the little woman told me. "Better take it and leave while I smooth her feathers down."

"They're married, " Tiffany whispered to me as she led me to the desk and handed me my check. "Can you believe they've been together for twenty-five years?"

I rubbed my aching shoulders. "True love," I guessed.

"All they do is fight, but Ronni is one of the best hairdressers in the business and when she's not flying off the handle, she's one of the sweetest women you'd wish to meet."

"I don't want to meet her on a bad day." I tried to shake the hurt out of my shoulders.

I sat in the car, shaking. I wished I still smoked because I could use something to calm my nerves. How could I have been so stupid as to just waltz in, turn on the charm and think I was going to waltz out, unscathed? Sooner or later, someone was going to kill the messenger, and that meant me. I looked in the rearview mirror at the bruises on my face.

***

I'd been threatened a few times as a reporter, usually with arrest for trespassing or a lawsuit for libel, but without much of a leg to stand on or after an estimate for billable hours from a lawyer, people always backed down.

Time to take stock.

Con. I was getting hit, threatened and subjected to unpleasantness. Yesterday's special guests had included the police. And after it was all over but the shouting, I learned the court order should be served by a pro, in a public place so the mom wouldn't run off with the kid and head for the border. A very ugly custody battle with a mom with mental health issues, a terrified dad and me serving papers, which is a job usually done by retired police officers. In my mind, I revisited the scene. It was an ugly blur and I decided I wanted to keep it that way. I hoped they kept the mom in the pych unit past the 72 hour hold. Again today, I'd been threatened with bodily harm. Whoever said 'kill the messenger' was right.

Pro. Okay. Delivering bad news was paying off. Not that there were any gold shower curtains or Porsche SUV's in my future, but the bills were getting paid, I was able to make a decent contribution to the Santimoke Gazette fund, and with my unemployment about to run out, I was secure in a month-to-month fashion, as long as I didn't buy new clothes or add premium channels to my cable, or buy steak.

But I knew it couldn't last. It was getting old for one thing and unpleasant for another. No one likes the bearer of bad news, and I'd been called more ugly names than a political candidate. One of these days, I was pretty sure someone was going to go off and kill me. I needed to get out, but how?

Happily, Susan had invited Finn and me to have lunch aboard *Miss Mindie* or I would have gone home, stayed in bed and pulled the covers up over my head. It was nice to see her so happy, and when I hugged her, she smelled faintly of a floral scent.

"What happened to you?" she asked, looking at my bruises. "You look as if you've been beaten up."

"I was struck by an angry white woman who didn't like the papers I was delivering. After that, an angry black woman pushed me around like a rag doll. It's a couple of stories, but they can wait until I've had a glass of something. It's been a long couple of days."

She looked at me, her dark eyes quizzical. "Someone's had a rough time. You need a glass of wine."

"Maybe a couple glasses of wine," I sighed, watching as she opened a bottle of something that probably cost more than my unemployment check.

"So, what happened at the hospital?" Finn asked me as he came in and washed his hands. He looked at my face quizzically. "Did you slip by the Black Bombshell and take care of the bad breath lady from church?"

"So much has happened you wouldn't believe it," I told him and Susan. "In fact, I'm not sure I believe it myself."

While I told them my long, sad story about the crazy ladies and the return of the native, Susan bustled about, ladling cold cucumber soup and slicing tekkamaki.

"It's so hot, I'd thought I'd do a cold lunch. We can eat on the lounge deck. It's got air and we can still get a nice view of the Bay." She gestured around with the knife. "I never thought I'd find a boat like this. And the owner's this really cool guy. He only uses her in the winter. He wants me to cook for him when he goes to the islands this winter. Then maybe across the Atlantic to the Mediterranean in the spring."

"And she'd give up sanding teak for a job like that?" Finn said, grinning.

I had a feeling they might be developing a thing. Something could have happened since the night Miss Wilsie went down and I'd missed my chance. And they did have a lot in common. I thought the way they smiled at each other said something was going on, and I felt disappointed.

I tried not to stare at Finn's torso straining against his tee, or feel a faint sense of envy because I'd kind of created all this possible happiness and no good deed goes unpunished.

"I definitely would give up sanding teak," Susan was saying. "I've had enough cold weather to last me a lifetime. And we'll be in touch. I'll be flying back to Maryland once in a while, and you'll be flying down to the Islands. And there's Skype and Facetime and. . ."

"Yep. But it won't be the same, babe." He reached for a piece of tekkamaki and she playfully slapped his hand, but not so hard he dropped his tuna roll.

"Smudge a little wasabi on that,"

she commanded. "Give it some bite." She refilled my wine. "Honestly, Marianna, I don't know how to thank you. If it weren't for you, I'd probably still be living in my car."

"You're the woman who fixes everyone's problems," Finn added, popping himself a beer. He hummed a few bars of a hymn. Choir practice tonight. I admired Finn's faith, but more than that, I admired the kind of gospel they featured in his mostly African American church. I wished I had faith in something.

No one asked me who fixed my problems, I thought, in a brief flash of self-pity that I quickly stowed away.

"How's your neighbor?" Finn asked, and I shifted into storytelling gear, filling them in on the latest adventures.

"It's like a soap opera," Finn remarked. "I mean the return of the prodigal son, I mean daughter. That's going to be interesting, that whole transgender thing." He took a swig of beer.

"But I don't like the look of those bruises. Seriously, Marianna, this bad news delivery service might have started as something fun, but it could get dangerous. I'm going to have to tell that lady at my church she needs to give you all the information next time. I'm sorry. If I'd known, I would have warned you off the job. You don't know how crazy people can be. You really need to be more careful."

"No, you don't know how crazy people can be," Susan agreed. "My ex-husband started out sane and charming and turned into a monster before I understood just how violent and disturbed he could be."

"Oh, I'll be careful," I promised. "Next time someone approaches me with papers to serve, I'll leave it to the cops. I thought it was easy money. But it turned ugly fast."

The conversation drifted away from me and on to boatyard matters.

Susan was talking about staying on the boat when the owner took her down the Inland Waterway and on to the Islands. Of course, there'd be a full crew, and no doubt a lot of guests. Maybe I could become a boat bum. I needed a career change, it seemed. Life was suddenly feeling like a shoe that looks good in the store but pinches when you wear it at home. A change of venue would do me some good.

Chapter Sixteen

As I walked back to my car, I ruminated. Maybe, like my favorite noire detective, Philip Marlowe, I needed life insurance. I needed a vacation. I needed a place in the country. I needed a new job. But all I had was a metaphorical hat, a coat and a gun. I metaphorically put them on and went out the metaphorical door.

And I needed a reason to feel less lonely. Sure, the men had come and the men had gone. There'd even been that brief disastrous marriage back the day. It was a mixed marriage. I was human, he was Klingon. I had lots of friends, including close women friends, but most of them were married and most of them had kids. Single and childless might have bought me some freedom, but it also brought feelings of aloneness.

The moment of self- pity and

doubt passed with a sigh, and I focused on the work at hand, which was stopping at the drugstore, the grocery store and the dry cleaners. Life is full of sadness and regret and it will eat you alive, if you let it, but you still have to buy toilet paper and pick up your good silk pants from Waterside Dry Cleaning.

I drove home. The sun was casting long shadows across the lawns, and the heat rose from the back alley in tiny mirages. I parked my ancient, dented car in the old garage, where Jamey's rented BMW gleamed in the shade. I barely noticed a black SUV with tinted windows parked down the alleyway. People were always parking in the alley, but that was a strange car. Maybe visiting.

The back garden lay baking in the sun. The cupid fountain spilled water in a trickle for a few thirsty birds, and the daylilies were blooming. Since Jamey's arrival, even the overgrown grounds had taken on a new life, thanks to his attentions. The scent of the ancient wisteria hung in the air and the brick pathway had been weeded and reset. The mockingbird that lived in the magnolia tree sang loudly as I opened the door to my place.

I'd tried to give Jamey and Miss Wilsie some privacy to catch up. I'd stick my head in the door for a minute or so to deliver the mail, only to be invited in almost every night for one of Jamey's cocktails and tales of her adventures on the Left Coast.

As Miss Wilsie and I listened, she spun some great stories. She seemed to know everyone, and everyone knew her. Some of her stories concerned little known facts about well- known people, which of course, fascinated us. She was a wonderful raconteur, and completely charming. I started to adore her as much as Miss Wilsie. And I trusted my instincts that she loved her grandmother.

As I let myself into the house, Jamey stuck a freshly champagned blonde head out the door. Gold and turquoise earrings of utter fabulousness, as she would say, dangled at her jawline. I caught a glimpse of a floral print tunic.

She beckoned to me with a hand glittering with hot pink nails. She was a better woman than I could ever hope to be. She had the whole feminine thing down. Once again, happy for you, but what about me?

"There you are, darling girl! We haven't seen you in days. Come in and have an iced tea with us. It's hellishly hot."

As I waltzed into Miss Wilsie's room, two smiling faces turned to greet me. Miss Wilsie was dressed in a beautiful blue caftan with just a smidge of mascara and eyeshadow, sporting a terrific new haircut that made her look 20 years younger. She waved her hot pink nails at me.

"We have the most exciting news, dear!" She leaned slightly so I could kiss her cheek, which was surprisingly smooth and unwrinkled. I really had to find out what Jamey's secrets were.

Jamey turned from the bar. "One Long Island Iced Tea, and two fresheners. L'chaim, ladies!" I was presented with a very welcome cold drink. It was of course, delicious. Jamey served her grandmother, then settled herself. "Yes. At least I'm hoping you think it's good news," she said. "You've been Grammy's friend and caretaker for so long, we really want your blessing for our project."

"Marianna," Miss Wilsie announced in her most thrilling tones, "I'm blowing this popsicle stand and going to California with Jamey. I've got a few good years left, and I intend to live them to the fullest."

Jamey grinned. "Isn't it great? The LGBT community is going to adore her. It's about time Grammy had some fun."

"To a new life!" Miss Wilsie held up her glass. "These dear people need me!"

And she needed them, I thought. She needed an adoring audience. It was only her due.

Chapter Seventeen

Jamey poured with a heavy hand. I took a deep swallow of my drink and leaned back into the sofa cushions, feeling the cold liquid sliding down my throat, soothing my parched soul.

It wasn't until later that I realized there would be changes, and how much I hate change. But that moment, I was just happy for both of them. They were like a pair of conspiring middle schoolers.

"I've got a great house in Marin County. It overlooks Bodega Bay. She'll love it, and I'll love having her with me. I've missed you so much, Grammy." Jamey patted Miss Wilsie's hand with a wrist full of turquoise bangles.

"I still can't believe you're alive. I can't believe Fred did this to me," Miss Wilsie's jaw tightened in a way that did not bode well for Fred. "Did this to you,

Jamey. Just cut you off and pretended...well!"

"Grammy, Dad did what he thought was best. Now, it was twisted, cruel and about as far from Christian as you can get, but in his tiny little mind, it was best. For him. As far as he was concerned, I was Satan. They couldn't handle the, the disgrace of it all. A lot of families were like that. Still are." Jamey's tone was matter of fact, but his fingers opened and closed into fists. "Years of therapy," he informed us slowly. "Years and years of therapy."

"But you could have told me, Jamey," Miss Wilsie said, holding Jamey's fingers to still them. "I had a feeling you were different when I saw you trying on my hats and my jewelry." She stroked his cheek with her other hand. "Male or female or something in between, you're still my Jamey, and oh, how I missed you. It's a miracle you've come back to me." She smiled mistily.

"I didn't think I could tell anyone back then. I was so confused and so ashamed. I should have been in touch,

Grammy. But I didn't think you'd accept me as a woman. I should have known better. We've got so much catching up to do. You're going to love California. And California is going to love you." He grinned at her fondly. "You're going to have so much fun with the community."

Miss Wilsie shrugged, dabbing at her eyes. "This is the happiest day of my life. I used to lie here and ask God to take me. Almost all my friends are dead, and the ones that aren't ought to be. They've given up. I thought I was past my usefulness, no Marianna, don't say anything. But now, I've got a whole new reason to live!" Color flooded her cheeks and her eyes sparkled. "When do we leave, Jamey?"

"The sooner the better, as far as I'm concerned," Jamey said. "The last thing I want to do is run into my parents. They're liable to beat me to death with a Bible." He laughed.

"You let me handle them," Miss Wilsie commanded him. "I've got a thing or two to say to that lot."

"Miss Wilsie!" I exclaimed. I

was having doubts. For all that Jamey seemed like an affable guy, I mean girl, she'd only been around for a week or so, and all we knew about her was what she said herself. My reporter cynicism was kicking in. I couldn't help it. Years of sourcing every statement made suspicion an ingrained habit. Jamey could be Mother Theresa, and I'd still wonder. "I mean, this is so sudden. Shouldn't you think it over? Moving to California is a big step to take. And what about your doctors and your meds and your..."

"There are doctors aplenty in California, I'm sure," Miss Wilsie said. "I'm going." She had that imperious look on her face that meant The Dowager Empress not only wasn't going to budge, she was not amused.

"But you hardly know this guy, I mean girl." Gender pronouns were never my strong suit and I knew I had a lot to learn.

"Feel free to check me out. Google, whatever. I have plenty of references," Jamey said with a very disarming grin. "And an excellent credit rating."

"Well, I'm going and that's that." Miss Wilsie had a whim of iron. "I know my own grandson, I mean daughter. I'd know her anywhere. I'm going. Which leaves you, Marianna, with one last job for me."

I shook my head and threw up my hands.

"Oh, no. Oh, no. I'm not doing that. My days as the bearer of bad news are over. I was attacked by an insane woman and almost clocked by an angry hairdresser who looked like she belonged on the starting line of the Caps. No, no more bad news for me. We're gonna get the paper up online and that's that. No more."

Miss Wilsie shushed me imperiously. "You're to wait until I'm on the plane and then you're going to tell Fred and Myrtle I'm long gone. And what's more, you're going to tell them they're out of my will. But you're going to wait until we're in the air, remember."

"I'm renting us a private jet,"

Jamey explained. "We can leave whenever Grammy is ready."

"Oh, no. Just no!" I protested. "You need to tell them yourselves. Miss Wilsie, I'm out of the bad news business as of this morning. Fred and Myrtle will throw me out of the back apartment, and sue me for something, but I'm still not telling them anything."

Still, I hadn't seen Miss Wilsie this happy in years. Losing my apartment was a small price to pay for her happiness. I could always find a new place to live. Miss Wilsie didn't have a lot of time left, and she deserved to spend what she had being the center of an adoring crowd of admirers.

"To us!" Jamey raised a glass and we all toasted.

Chapter Eighteen

"**A**m I interrupting something?" A hatchet-faced woman in a pantsuit and pearls knocked on the door jamb. She didn't look any too thrilled. Her red lips were pressed together tightly. "I've been knocking on the front door but no one answered. So I used my authority to let myself in and check on you." She looked from one to the other of us as if we were mice and she'd just discovered us in her underwear drawer. Nice.

I didn't know authority was a passkey. Where could I get one? Fortunately, I didn't say it out loud.

"Mrs. Chively! What a surprise! This is my grand, uh, daughter, Jamey, and my, er caregiver Marianna. Mrs. Chively is the dictator, I mean director of Adult Protective Services at the hospital." Miss Wilsie gestured. "I suppose you have some papers I need to sign. Marianna, get my checkbook, will you, dear?"

"Mrs. Sharpless, I came to check up on you," Mrs. Chively said as she came into the room uninvited. "You checked out against medical advice. And your doctors were concerned."

"Indeed I did. I was ready to come home, and as you can see, I am not alone here. Furthermore, I am going to live with Jamey in California. I want to spend the time I have left with someone who loves me, not my money. And I will remind you that I have been a substantial benefactor to the hospital over the years." Oh, she was majestic when she wanted to be. I wanted to be just like her when I grew up.

Mrs. Chively smiled a frosty smile that didn't quite reach her eyes.

Wow, was she over-accessorized, I noticed in the dead, uncomfortable silence that followed. Designer scarf, big gold eagle pin, those pearls, big solid gold earrings, diamond wrist watch, and a couple of rings with stones you could use as a skating rink. Obviously, her mother had never taught her to get completely dressed, and then remove one piece of jewelry.

"You know, you shouldn't check out against medical advice, and Dr. Rothrock really doesn't think you should travel," she said in that same tone of voice Mrs. Dean, my high school principal had used when she caught me smoking in the girl's room. "Haven't we done everything to make you comfortable at the hospital? Private suite, meals delivered from Out of the Fire? Private C.N.A.'s? We have a lovely assisted living facility..."

"To the tune of three grand a week," Miss Wilsie replied, drawing herself up majestically. "That ward is like an expensive warehouse for people who are waiting to die. I thought I was waiting to die, but now I realize I very much want to live with my Jamey. California sounds like a wonderful place to spend my last years."

"I am planning on taking

excellent care of her," Jamey drawled. But there was a dangerous undercurrent. "She'll have twenty-four-hour care on call, her own suite in my house with a fabulous view of Bodega Bay, and a host of people, who when they meet her, are going to become her adoring admirers. And of course," she added. "The very best health care. I'm not without resources myself."

She'd inherited her grandmother's style, all right. Miss Wilsie herself could not have been more imperious.

It looked as if we were going to have a standoff right here. I had enough sense not to open my mouth, but that didn't mean I wasn't watching the showdown. I waited to see who would blink first.

Mrs. Shively clutched her pearls. Miss Wilsie glared. Jamey moved protectively toward her grandmother. She might have been transitioned, but she was still six feet tall and powerfully built.

"I called..." Mrs. Chively started

to threaten, but at that moment Bad News walked in the door. "You need to be protected. . ." she finished lamely, but no one heard her.

"Momma, what's going on here?" Fred and Myrtle barged into the room as if they owned it. Fred was bellowing, and Myrtle, good, obedient spouse that she was, was making little mews of distress.

"Jamey, what are you doing here? Why are you wearing women's clothes?" It's a wise mother who knows her own child, transgendered or not.

"You're an abomination before the Lord. Get out, get out!" Fred swelled up like a bald toad. His little glasses glittered, and his tiny hands waved in the air. He looked at his son with fear and loathing, and slowly turned a bright scarlet. "You!" he snarled in tones of loathing. "How dare you?"

Now, I thought, we are going to have some fun.

I was hoping Fred would have a massive heart attack then and there.

Selfishly, I also realized I was relieved of any obligation to deliver Fred and Myrtle any bad news.

Myrtle, who outweighed Fred by fifty pounds and towered over him by several inches, cooed and mewed. I was hoping she would faint. How could you abandon your own child like that? She had earned my unbridled contempt with her spinelessness.

Mom and Dad stared at Jamey. Jamey lifted her head and stared back. You could have cut the air with the steel in that stare. Myrtle's mews turned to a whine, and she dropped to her knees, her chubby hands clasped toward the crystal chandelier.

"Lord, deliver us from this demon in the form of our son! Jesus, I pray you remove this Satan from our midst!"

"Oh, shut up, Myrtle," Miss Wilsie snapped. "I'm tired of you. You were a fool when you were a girl, you're a fool now, and I won't be unhappy never to see you again. And as for you,

Fred Sharpless, you'd better pray to Jesus for lying to me about my own grandson all these years, because if I could get a hold of my cane, I'd beat you senseless! You were a nasty, sneaky, greedy little boy, and you're a nasty, greedy, lying little man, just like your father! Would you care to explain to me how you let this happen?"

Fred, who looked like a rockfish at the best of times, opened and closed his mouth. He should have been on ice at the fish store. His face turned as white as a sheet.

"Filthy sinner! How dare you come back and upset Mother? You may not be physically dead, but your perverted lifestyle has made you dead to us! Shameful! Son of Satan! I have no son, and haven't for years! How dare you..."

"Return from the dead? Ruin your respectable finger quotes "Christian" life? Become what I was born to be, a woman? You disgust me, Fred. I can't even call you Dad. Or you Mom, Myrtle. You're as guilty as he is because you stood by and watched him beat the shit out of me. And lie, lie to Grammy and tell me she would rather see me dead than a woman." Jamey's voice was level, but he was angry. And he had a lot to be angry about.

"This whole transgender thing is too complicated for them to understand," Miss Wilsie said. "They don't read."

"Jesus will punish you!" Fred quavered. "You will burn in the eternal fire of Hell."

"Now, I do have to say something," I put in. "Mistaking your personal opinion for God's will is pure blasphemy. At least that's what I think."

"You stay out of this! You've been a bad influence on Mother since the day you moved in! I bet you had something to do with this!" Fred turned to me, his mustache quivering with righteous indignation.

I shrugged. "Not my circus, not my monkeys. As ye sow, so shall ye reap." Mixing clichés is my hobby.

"Now that Jamey's back," Miss

Wilsie said, I'm going to California with him and end my days in peace and quiet, as far away from you as I can get. You betrayed me, you betrayed Jamey, you betrayed the family. And you pretend to be such a fine, fine Christian!"

"He just wants your money. He's a demon! A sinner! A- - - a sodomite!"

"Actually, I'm a transsexual. A post-operative transsexual," Jamey pointed out calmly. "I am a woman. And, yes, I came back to get my only loving relative to take her home where someone loves her, not her money. Believe me, I have plenty of my own. Your greed is one of the things I didn't inherit, Fred."

Fred's eyes bulged out of his head. "I'll get a lawyer! I'll have Mother declared incompetent! I'll get power of attorney!"

"Don't forget the hospital's yearly donation!" Mrs. Shively put in. She was doing more pearl clutching throughout this ugly scene, and I had the feeling she couldn't wait to the yacht club and tell all her friends about it.

"The scandal," Myrt moaned and sank into a chair. "Oh, what will they say at church? I'll be the talk of the church basement!"

"I'm calling the police! You're disturbing other residents," Mrs. Chively said. "I'll tell them you're exercising undue influence on a poor old woman."

"Actually, we're giving them a great show," I pointed out. "There hasn't been this much excitement on Water Street since Mrs. Cauffman caught Mrs. Draft and Mr. Cauffman doing the nasty in the boxwoods."

"I'll go with you," Fred said. "We'll put a stop to this foolishness. I'll have Mother declared senile! We'll hold her in protective custody. I'll call Judge Hughes."

"Just you try! Jimmy Hughes has been trying to get me to marry him for years!" Miss Wilsie exclaimed. "Now all of you get out of here. Except you Jamey, and you, Marianna. You stay." She pointed to the door. "Out! And don't let the door hit you on the way out! Out, all of you! Out! Or I'll call the police! I'll call that nice young man who comes by to make sure the doors are locked at night! He'll take care of the pack of you!"

"You can't do this!" Fred sputtered. "I have my rights!"

"And I have a judge, the police chief and a landshark lawyer on speed dial, so make a move," I challenged, waving my iPhone in the air. A reporter is nothing without her sources.

"People will talk! They're already talking," Myrt moaned. "Oh, Lord Jesus, save me!"

"You haven't heard the last of us! This is elder abuse!" Mrs. Chively snapped, straightening out her pearls. "I'll get a writ and have her declared non compos mentis!"

"And I'll assume guardianship," Fred asserted. "You've been deluded by Satan, Momma. You don't know what you're doing!"

"Oh, Lord! I feel faint!" Myrtle exclaimed, throwing her hands up in the air so her Ethel Mermans flapped in the breeze.

"It's probably just a hot flash, Myrt," I pointed out.

Fred and Mrs. Chively practically had to drag her down the hall, no mean feat since Myrtle weighed close to three hundred pounds. But Jamey gave them an escort, and who would fight with him?

Miss Wilsie collapsed back in her chair. I thought she was going to have a spasm, but she was laughing like I hadn't heard her laugh in years. "Oh, that was wonderful! That was just wonderful! Oh, thank you, Jamey, my love! My hero! You saved me from those dreadful people!"

I drained my drink. I needed it after that. "Wow." I managed to say. "Wow."

"Okay," Jamey said, returning to the room and closing the door behind him. "We need to get Grammy out of here and fast. Fred's capable of anything, as long as there's money involved. And as long as the hospital is collecting three grand a month from Grammy, that bitch witch is going to help him."

"We could take her to my house," I suggested.

Miss Wilsie shook her head. "That's the first place they'll look."

A hotel? A motel? A bed and breakfast?" Jamey wondered. He was already looking in the closets for Miss Wilsie's bags. "When we get to California, Grammy, I'm buying you a whole new wardrobe. This stuff is positively dowdy. Polyester? Tell me this is not rayon polyester." He held up a blouse as if it were roadkill.

"I have an idea!" I exclaimed. It was just like a light bulb went off over my head. "I have a friend who caretakes this enormous yacht. It's huge, and there's more than enough room for the entire Russian army. And no one would ever think of looking for us in a boatyard."

I took out my cell phone and punched in Susan's number.

Twenty minutes later, the Beemer backed out of the garage, headed through the night to Spruce Boatworks, the last place anyone would look for a runaway granny and her loving granddaughter.

As I saw them off, I noticed the black SUV was still parked in the alley. Since no one was jumping out of it to apprehend any of us, I ignored it. As soon as they left, I locked all the doors and turned on the burglar alarms. We hadn't needed them for years, I reflected grimly. And now we need them to keep out family.

Life is a strange train.

Chapter Nineteen

I t was a dark and stormy night.

No seriously, it was.

A rainy front had moved in from the northeast, bringing fog and a sullen downpour that never seemed to let up.

Another Wednesday night at the Lucky Duck, another Santimoke Gazette meeting. I got there late because I had some other things to do, like help Jamey rent a jet out of our local airport. I just happened to know Muffy and Skipper, who had enough money to actually own a small jet. A couple of phone calls, and their pilot would be ready to fly to the left coast when the weather cleared enough to fly. If it was Miss Wilsie, they were good with it, especially when they heard the whole story. Fred wasn't going to win any Miss Congeniality awards around here. And with Jamey and Miss

Wilsie safely and secretly installed aboard *Miss Mindie* until they could escape, I was content that I'd nailed down that problem.

So I breezed into the bar, a little out of breath and wet from the rain. I'd had to park at the house, blocks away and run through the puddles to get here. The black SUV was parked in front of the Duck. Somebody got around. I was a little startled to see a strange man seated at what I thought of as our table at the Duck. He smelled strongly of law enforcement or the military, what with the stone face and the brush cut and the humorless eyes.

Normally, I wouldn't care about the guy, but circumstances being that they were, my reporter radar was up and I took my seat cautiously.

"Marianna, this is Sergeant Alan Brieland," Stu said, and I could hear the unease he was trying to conceal. "He's been looking for you. He's from Alaska."

The hair on the back of my neck stood up, and the first thing I thought about was protecting Susan. Shit, shit, shit.

The waitress brought me my beer, and it gave me time to sip it and look him over. His smile, full of teeth, never reached his eyes. He didn't offer to shake my hand and I didn't offer it. I felt the crazy all around him, and my palms began to sweat.

I was aware of everyone staring at me. I had a flash that they'd throw me under the bus in a New York minute, then dismissed it. They only knew what I had told them, and I hadn't told them much more than I needed to explain my checks. Client confidentiality. No one knew the whole Susan story, although they would have been blind not to see me hanging around Finn. I wished he was here now, but it was Wednesday, and he was still at choir practice.

"Ms. Trench, I'm looking for someone. I traced her down to the Eastern Shore. Your cell phone showed up on her records, and we thought you might be able to help us locate her."

The stalker husband. Shit, shit,

shit. Could this be him? Just looking at him scared me.

"And you are?" I asked in my best Miss Wilsie, grand dowager voice.

He pulled some stuff out of his pocket. Alaska State Police ID and some other papers. A badge. Allegedly, a sergeant in the Alaska State Police, based in Seward. The photo matched the ID, but I knew a guy over in Delaware who could make me everything from a fake social security number to a phony passport for the right price.

"How may I help you?" I asked, holding on to his stuff. My crew was just looking at me, waiting to see what would happen. If I was expecting backup, I was wrong. Dead wrong. They had no clue.

His jaw tightened. He looked at me like I was a wolf he was going to shoot from a plane. I looked back at him as if I had several million dollars and an exalted parade of ancestors backing me up. Miss Wilsie would be proud.

"I'm looking for Susan Korsakoff. We traced her here. She calls you from her cell. You know her?"

"Never heard of her. You sure you got the right person?" I can lie like a rug. Years of practice have made me an expert.

"Well, she seems to know you, according to the phone calls we traced." His smile never reached those shark eyes. He would have made a great Grand Inquisitor.

Damn, I thought, why didn't she buy a burner? Maybe she did. Who knows what resources he could tap into? "Exactly why are you looking for this person?" I wished I had a reporter notebook to whip out. Making notes scares people.

"She's wanted in Alaska for drug dealing. Moving a lot of meth."

"Allegedly," Stu put in automatically. "According to the Associated Press Stylebook, you need to say allegedly if she hasn't been convicted. Otherwise, she can sue you."

"Slander," I suggested helpfully. "Or if you print it, libel."

I pulled out my cell phone and punched in a contact, squinting at his ID.

"What are you doing?" Brieland asked. I'd thrown him off, just a little. So he wasn't invincible and I wasn't helpless.

"I'm calling the Santimoke County sheriff to check your bona fides. You did check in with local law enforcement, didn't you?"

"Concurrent jurisdiction is big in Maryland," Jimmy pointed out helpfully.

Brieland snarled something so obscene even I can't repeat it and snatched his papers and badge out of my hands. We all watched in silence as he stomped out the door.

I shut the phone off. "I think that answers my question," I said. Why bother Sheriff Greene when she was eating dinner? And what if I was wrong and he was legit?

"Want to tell us what's going on?" Stu asked.

"I could tell you, but then I'd

have to kill you," I laughed, but inside I wasn't laughing at all.

I was sort of half there and half not there through the staff meeting. What did I know about Susan Korsakoff, anyway, except what she had told me? What if she was on the run from the law? She didn't look like a meth head, or act like one. No tracks, no jitters, no wild ideas. Of course, a lot of dealers didn't do their own product. On the other hand, an obsessed control freak, even one who was a cop, especially one who was a cop, was capable of anything to get a runaway woman back. Stalking, for instance.

I felt a cold sweat breaking out along my back and my hands were shaking. This guy had scared me. Scared me a lot. I needed to make a call, but I didn't dare if he had a wire on the line.

I barely listened to the sports scores or glanced at the photos of grip and grins to go into the next issue. If there were weddings and engagements, I didn't care. If the Watertown Lions kicked the daylights out of the Easton

Warriors at baseball, well, good for them. As long as my name wasn't in the obits, what did I care?

Just as I thought the meeting was over, it went into extra innings because Jimmy had questions about the layout of the sports pages on line. After ten minutes of ledes, gutters and widows, I was ready to scream. My palms were sweating and that third beer wasn't going down well.

When I finally got outside, the wind had whipped up, and the rain was coming down in sheets. I could barely see the streetlights and the dim illumination from the closed stores. The street was deserted. Not a fit night for man or beast, as my father said. Why hadn't I moved to Florida when Mom and Dad retired? I could be living in Islamorada right now, floating on the blue water. Instead of being dead afraid. The irony was that someone had handed me a piece of bad news and I didn't know what to do with it. Calling local police was a bad idea. Of course they'd believe him before they believed me, and by the time they'd figured out he was dirty, it would be too late.

I waddled through the puddles back to my car, which was now standing in a pool of water. Even as I started the engine, turned on the wipers and the lights and buckled myself in, I knew what I was going to do.

Stupid me.

Chapter Twenty

The fog thickened as I drove, and there was almost no traffic on the road. In several places, the two lane blacktop was flooded, spilling out of the ditches and onto the road. It must have been close to ten or eleven by the time I got to Spruce Boatworks.

The security gates were closed and locked for the night, but I pushed 911 on the lock, and they slid open for me. The fog was so dense I couldn't see my hand in front of my face. Snatches and patches of smoke drifted like ghosts and the wind was blowing the rain in sheets.

I kind of felt my way inside, in the dark. You could barely see the security lights, just dim yellow spots in the darkness. I could hear, but not see the shrouds clanging against the mastheads of boats. It was like forlorn music in the night. I'd always rather liked the sound, but tonight it seemed ominous and threatening. I could barely make out familiar buildings and shapes in the grey blackness until I was almost on top of a shed or a hull up in the stands. I'd never seen a fog as thick this.

The car crawled between the buildings and the boats, which loomed large and ominous out of the darkness and the mist. Almost by instinct, I parked at the foot of the dock where *Miss Mindie* was moored. Lights were dim in the lounge and the staterooms, so I figured Jamey and Miss Wilsie were on board. I mounted the causeway and made my way up the gangplank to the deck.

Too late, I saw the black SUV parked by the catwalk, nearly invisible through the mist and rain. The ride of Brieland, the dirty cop. He'd tracked Susan.

The shock of something pulling tightly around my neck was so sudden and unexpected it threw me off balance. I gasped for air.

"Got you now, you stupid bitch," a voice snarled in my ear, and I knew it was Brieland. "Led me right to her!"

Somehow, he'd tailed me here.

I tried to pry his arm off my neck, but it was impossible. His arms were huge and solid. I tried reaching back and kicking him in the scrotum, but he lifted me off the deck, so I was dangling in midair, gasping for breath.

He swung me, and suddenly, I was falling a long way down. I managed to screech as I fell, but if anyone inside heard me, it would have been a miracle.

I hit the water in a cannonball. It was warm from summer, but I plunged downward until I hit muddy bottom. I started to struggle for the surface, but my clothes weighed me down. I kicked off my sandals and then realized it was so dark I didn't know which way was up. I couldn't feel bottom anymore.

I was running out of air and completely disoriented. Then I remembered to watch my air bubbles. Air bubbles are lighter than water, and head to the surface. In an emergency, you do what you've been trained to do. Even though it was dark, I could still feel them rise, and pushed myself up in their direction. I broke the surface, inhaled a deep breath and was mad as fire.

Furious with myself for leading Brieland to Susan, enraged that I'd put my friends in danger from a crazy man, just pissed as hell at the hand life had dealt me. It was all converging into one giant ball of rage. I came up by the smooth hull of the boat, where I couldn't find a purchase.

To make it worse, jellyfish were draping their long, stinging tentacles all over me, and that really hurt. Their tentacles draped over my head, stinging my eyes.

I tried to reach out for the catwalk, but it was too far away. The barnacles on the piling scraped my hand. I remembered there was a diving platform on the back of the yacht. I began to feel my way along the hull, making my way toward the stern, sputtering and cursing and vowing revenge. I was too mad to be afraid, too busy scraping jellies off my face to plan ahead. I just knew I wanted retaliation.

I finally found the slippery diving platform, grabbed a railing and managed to pull myself up. I lay on the duckboards, catching my breath and de-stringing myself of nettles. Things could have been worse. If it had been winter, I would have died of hypothermia three minutes after I hit the winter. And I would have been dragged down by layers and layers of thick clothes. A tee-shirt and a pair of linen pants didn't add much weight, but I was going to miss those Nordstrom sandals on the bottom of the river.

Happily, the *Miss Mindie* was fully equipped with a ladder that went all the way from the platform to the main deck, and I peered around through the mist, the rain and a veil of red rage.

All I could hear was the rattle of raindrops and the distant drone of the TV in the lounge. Under the bulkhead, I searched for and found a gaffer hook, an essential piece of safety equipment on any vessel. And a nice weapon for a pissed-off woman.

My advantage was that I knew this boat better than Sergeant Brieland did. Wherever he went, it would be unknown territory to him, whereas I'd been over every inch of the place.

I hugged the cabin as I crept toward the lighted windows of the lounge. If I made any noise, the rain and wind would have drowned it out. At least I hoped. The wet teak deck was slippery. Thunder clapped overhead and it felt as if the whole boat rocked with the rumble.

I wasn't sure who was guilty or who was innocent, but a guy who doesn't check in with local law enforcement and throws a person overboard stands a pretty good chance of being the villain of the piece.

I peered through the trails of rain into the window. Sure enough, Miss Wilsie, Jamey and Susan were lined up on the couch while Brieland loomed over them. That really, really looked like a gun in his hand. I couldn't hear him, but I had a feeling he was gloating. The guy was truly crazy.

Well, shit, shit, shit.

I felt in my pocket for my phone, but it was gone, resting no doubt, at the bottom of the river between the catwalk and the hull, along with my expensive sandals. Finn and the workers were long gone, and the office and sheds were locked up. The nearest pay phone was up the road about a mile at a gas station.

How could I have been so stupid?

Now what?

I could burst through the door, gaff swinging, and disarm him, except the gaff was only about four feet long, and the hook wasn't more than six or eight inches. And he would turn and fire point blank the second he heard me come in.

Well, I could get shot, possibly killed, but it would give them time to disarm him while he was distracted with me.

Did I want to live forever?

As I was pondering that, Providence, divine or otherwise, decided to take a hand. Thunder clapped overhead. Or I thought it was thunder. Wrong. It was more like a herd of wild cattle stampeding.

While I watched open- mouthed, who should come up the gangway but Fred and Myrtle Sharpless, accompanied by a good part of what had to be the congregation of the Angry Jesus Church. Well, at least ten other indignant Christians. You could smell the indignation in the air.

They were like the villagers hunting for Frankenstein's monster. They had everything but torches and pitchforks. Happily, they couldn't see me in the dark, or they probably would have torched and pitch-forked me as they sang "Onward, Christian Soldiers" loud enough to awaken the dead. They clambered aboard the boat, good Christian pirates about to administer Angry Jesus justice to anyone who stood in the way of capturing a reluctant prize.

I had no idea what Fred had done to get them all worked up, but I could guess.

A   scary,   self-righteous   mob.

Chapter Twenty-One

"**H**ang on, Mother Wilsie! We're going to rescue you!" Myrt cried from beneath the plastic rain bonnet that covered her helmet hair. She must have gotten the call to arms while she was washing dishes. She was still wearing rubber gloves and her I HATE HOUSEWORK apron.

Fred rapped smartly on the door. "Mother, I know you're in there! Let me in! Open this door in the name of Jesus!"

"Mrs. Sharpless, this is Reverend Tyre! Cast out Satan and save your immortal soul!" A tall, thin man shouted through the door, shaking a plastic covered Bible as if it were a key that would open it. If I hadn't spent so much time around Fred and Myrtle, I wouldn't have believed real people talked like that, but there they were.

"Won't someone think of the children?" Myrt whined. "Mother Sharpless, you've disgraced us in front of the whole church!" That it was most decidedly not Miss Wilsie's Holy Trinity Episcopal made no difference.

There was a collective rumble from the congregation as they crowded around the door, shaking their Bibles and religious tracts. The ecstasy of drama was upon them. This was probably more exciting than a reality show, which is what I think most of them would have been home watching, if the telephone tree hadn't been put to use.

This was probably more excitement than they had since Eulalia Price had seen a vision of Christ in the back of the Church on the Sunday after Thanksgiving.

I couldn't quite see what was going on inside through a porthole, but it looked as if everyone was puzzled and surprised, even Brieland. The hostage situation seemed to have been temporarily forgotten as a howling mob of crazed senior Christians demanded admittance.

"Jesus, I beg of you, open this door! Destroy this evil inside!" Fred put his shoulder against the door and turned the knob. The church mob was almost on top of him. You would have thought it was a revival meeting and this was an altar call.

The door swung open. It wasn't even locked. Suddenly the entire congregation, no longer obstructed, fell through the door in a large clump of big blue hair, wrinkles and the smell of VapoRub.

"What the fu..." Brieland's gun wavered uncertainly as two bony women in pink plastic raincoats were pushed from behind, lost their balance and grasped uncertainly for support from the closest stable object, which was Brieland himself.

"We're here to save you, Wilsie!" One of them cried as she gripped Brieland's arm, the one with the gun. Of course, she had no idea he was carrying. Indeed, I'm not sure the congregation took in any of the situation, or if they even understood that Miss Wilsie most emphatically did not want to be rescued. From Jamey, at least.

"Young man, have you found Jesus?" the other lady asked Brieland as she steadied herself on his shoulder.

"Jesus, lady, I - - -"Brieland exclaimed irreverently.

"Oh thank God!" The lady cried. "Then help us save this poor old woman from the clutches of this sinful man!"

That was when the gun flew out of his hand and skidded across the deck. No one seemed to notice the firearm as the congregation righted themselves with great difficulty. You could almost hear the ancient joints cracking. I actually felt bad for them.

From my vantage point outside the porthole, I had a pretty good view of the action. But it was all happening so fast I could barely keep up. I wanted someone to pick up that gun. Someone not Brieland.

The congregation was still trying to find their feet. They weren't young, after all, and being mostly law-abiding citizens with a mild religious mania, weren't used to being out in rainstorms and fog, breaking into luxury yachts. They were certainly confused. Miss Wilsie didn't seem to be in any distress. As a matter of fact, she seemed furious with them for causing a scene.

They were finding out what I'd discovered weeks ago. No good deed goes unpunished.

I figured out that Fred had told them Miss Wilsie was being held captive by Jamey, that Abomination. He'd gotten them all riled up and away from a quiet, rainy evening at home. They were credulous and easily lead, and he was certainly capable of anything to keep the Sharpless money from slipping from his greedy grip.

While Brieland was trying to regain his balance, Jamey came at him with all the ruthlessness of a linebacker.

"I might be a woman," she roared, "But I sure as hell ain't a lady!"

I don't think Brieland knew what hit him. Mr. Snakeyes went down and took two church ladies with him.

That was when I decided I needed to do something, and crawled through the door and around the poor, well-meaning congregation, around the wrestling match that was Brieland and Jamey, and around Miss Wilsie and Susan, still on the couch. Susan might have been in fear, but Miss Wilsie was fearless. Her eyes were snapping with fire, and she was clutching her cane in a way I wouldn't like if I'd crossed her.

"Thank you, Jesus!" Fred cried, waving his Bible in the air.

"Oh, shut up, Fred! " Reverend Tyre was helping a geriatric gentleman to his feet. I think it was beginning to sink into the good reverend's innocent soul that the congregation had been bamboozled.

I crawled over Myrt's plastic rain bonnet. She was hysterical, speaking in either tongues or Urdu. Another lady in polyester was rolling around on the floor, while Fred was trying, rather ineffectually to hit Brieland the Bad Cop over the head with his plastic covered Bible. "Out, Satan! Out!" He was screaming,

"That's the bad guy! That guy with the brush cut! Get him! Help Jamey hold him down!" I yelled as I pounced on the gun with the gaffing hook, dragging it toward me.

Two gentlemen of the congregation were happy to leave off prayer, and go to Jamey's assistance.

Susan was trying to lift Miss Wilsie bodily off the couch and toward safety, but Miss Wilsie didn't want to go.

"I'm perfectly fine, dear! Just let me get a good whack in with this cane!"

Fred, seeing this, grabbed Miss Wilsie and he and Susan had quite a tug of war over the dowager. Who, after the initial shock had settled down, wasn't having any of it.

"Come with me, mother! Eternal

salvation is yours!" Fred was yelling.

Miss Wilsie was, as always, equal to the challenge.

She took her cane and planted it smartly into Fred's jaw. His eyes rolled back in his head and he collapsed on the floor in a dead knockout.

"I've always wanted to do that," Miss Wilsie exclaimed. "Now, dear, don't you worry about me, I can take care of myself!"

She leaned forward and delivered a smarting blow to the Brieland's head. "The lord helps those who help themselves!" Miss Wilsie laid about her with great abandon, her diamond rings flashing in the light.

I'd never been more proud of her than I was right that moment, as she tripped up a WalMartian lady with that stick, sending the woman flying across several people who were rolling on the floor in religious ecstasy or just an inability to get back on their feet.

Jamey grunted as she lifted Brieland and body-slammed him into a wall. Sergeant Stalker hit the teak paneling and slid down to the deck like an eel. Before he could get on his feet again, Jamey had him pinned and was tying his arms and legs behind his back with a Hermes scarf. She stuffed a cocktail napkin into the dirty cop's potty mouth. "I used to be on the wrestling team in high school," she finished triumphantly, turning to protect Miss Wilsie from a phalanx of old church ladies who seemed to be rushing her in a Hail Mary pass.

"We'll rescue you, Wilsie!" they cried.

In her religious fervor, Myrt was beating Fred with the Bible and she was enjoying it entirely too much. I had a feeling she'd wanted to do that for years.

"We've come to rescue you, Wilsie!" One of the congregations cried as they tried a full frontal assault on her. "It's what Jesus would want!"

Wilsie brandished her cane. "Rescue this, Lou Jean!" She poked the other lady in her ample bosom.

"Everybody calm down!" Jamey yelled. "Calm down!!"

"Brothers and Sisters, stand down! This has all been a dreadful, dreadful mistake! Brother Fred has used us, I say *used* us to his own ends! Wilsie is not being held a prisoner! Stand down!"

"Don't listen to him!" Fred yelled. "It's for all of us!"

No one seemed to be listening, just brawling with each other and anyone else who crossed their path.

I guess if your life is that churchy, you do yearn for more action and less talk.

"Okay," I yelled, waving the gun at the ceiling since all weapons are loaded, "Everybody freeze!"

Just like a cop drama. Except I got a little too excited and actually pulled the trigger. There was a loud pop and a big hole appeared in the skylight above our heads. Someone screamed. I was staring horrified at the hole when the skylight opened, sprinkling glass below.

A figure in a white robe dropped through the skylight just as the fog cleared. It was enough for a bright full moon to bathe the sky behind the figure in a magical aura.

White robe, sandals, pale glow…

"It's Jesus! The rapture has come!" One of the congregation exclaimed, and there was a murmur as all action ceased. We must have been quite a tableau.

The figure in white landed nimbly on his feet and looked around.

"What the hell is going on here?" Finn McCall demanded, all tall, tanned and magnificently in charge. "I called the cops and they're on their way! Clean up your act! No parties on this boat! Someone's gonna have to pay to replace this skylight. Did I mention no guns?"

"It's the Archangel Michael!" Myrt exclaimed. "The rapture is here! Oh, praise Jesus, and me in this old house dress about to be carried up to heaven."

"Praise Jesus!" I muttered, not entirely irreverently.

"You must be Finn; the Finn Marianna was talking about. Not that I don't appreciate heavenly intervention," Jamey said drily, "But what the hell are you wearing?"

"And you must be Jamey." Finn grinned, holding out his hand. "It's dress rehearsal for choir at church. I sing baritone. I do have a life outside of this boatyard, you know."

"Halleluiah."

Chapter Twenty-Two

"So then," I said, "Somebody called the real cops and the Fish Cops and the Coast Guard and all hell broke loose." I took a swig of my Corona.

"I bet it did. Why didn't you tell us that guy was crazy?" Donna asked.

"Because he's in cahoots with all kinds of meth makers and heroin dealers in Wasilla. On the job and on the arm. No wonder Susan was terrified of him. If he's jacked up to drive across country, who knows what else he's capable of?"

"But how did he track her all the way to the Eastern Shore?" Stu asked.

Oh, I had 'em all in the palm of my hand tonight. All the Lucky Duck regulars were gathered around to hear the story, too. It was the talk of Watertown this week. Next week, something else would come up, but for now, I was the center of attention.

"He'd put a tracking device on her car. It's apparently the kind of thing car dealers use when they sell to someone with bad credit. That way, if the customer defaults, the repo guys can track down the car. Cops evidently use them too. But it didn't function all that well. He lost contact with her car when she hit the Lower 48. Then all of a sudden, the tracker started working again. He was obsessed with Susan. He couldn't let her go. I honestly believe he would have killed her if he had half a chance."

I heightened the tension by eating a fry, savoring it as I chewed. " He was worse than a dirty cop. He was a psycho dirty cop. Sheriff Wanda's got him down at the jail now, waiting for an extradition team from Juno to come and pick him up, and fighting with them about which state gets to try him first. He's in deep trouble. I don't know if they're gonna press charges on him here or not. It'll be funny, being a witness instead of a reporter if they do. What a creep."

The truth was, I was still shaking days later. I had nightmares where he was coming after me, trying to drown me in deep water, trying to shoot me. So I could imagine how Susan must have felt, must still feel with a monster like that after her. No wonder she'd been so terrified.

"So, what happened when the Angry Jesus Church people came storming through the door?"

"The holy spirit must have been on them pretty strong. They fell through the door like the stateroom scene in that Marx Brothers movie. If I hadn't been so scared, I would have laughed. They came to rescue Miss Wilsie, who didn't want to be rescued because she's frozen chosen and doesn't hold with a lot of backbiting in church, but instead they saved us all from a very unpleasant time. They were yelling and speaking in tongues and all fired up. If they thought Jamey Sharpless was going to Hell, you can just imagine what they had to say about a bad drug dealing cop threatening to shoot people. I guess they do have some standards." I shook my head.

"Myrt sat on Brieland until the real law got there. And the rest of 'em prayed for his immortal soul. I think he was glad to go to a nice quiet jail. But that kind of took the wind out of their sails, and when they realized Miss Wilsie wasn't going to change her mind, they kind of accepted it. Hours of sitting around while law enforcement questioned everyone tuckered them out. I think they all go to bed at eight." I thought back and chuckled. "What I will never forget was Finn dropping through the skylight. In his white choir robe, he did look kind of saintly. They thought he was an angel and this was the rapture. It added something to the fun until they figured out it was just him."

"How did they know where Miss Wilsie was?" Jimmy asked.

"Evidently, the guy who services the Lear jet belongs to their church, and he overheard the pilot talking to the owners. You can't keep a secret on the

Eastern Shore."

I was tired and burned out. Scratch a cynic and find a failed romantic. I could be dead. Happily, I was still here.

Yeah, yeah, yeah. I know what you're thinking and you're probably right.

But something intervened, the bad guy was defeated, the forces of karma and justice prevailed, and yes, say what you would about the Angry Jesus Church, the Lord does work in mysterious ways, His wonders to perform. They might not have saved Miss Wilsie and Jamey from the pits of Hell, if you could call a cushy life in a McMansion in Marin County the pits of Hell, but they saved us all from a whole world of hurt, and possibly untimely death. I needed to re-examine my theology. Not now, but at some time in the future. I had an appointment with God. My faith was being restored.

"So where is Susan now?" Donna asked, poking at her virtuous salad.

"She took off with Jamey and Miss Wilsie in the jet for Marin County. She's going to look after her while Jamey gets her settled in. I think she needed a break. She's had the toughest time of all of us. I can't imagine living in that kind of fear for that long. And course, there's the blue code. You can't get the cops after another cop. She had nothing to do with his meth connections. She didn't even know about them. He'd get high and beat the crap out of her. Then when he calmed down, he'd be all apologetic and loving and there'd be dramatic makeup sex, and, well, we've seen enough of it in court. Domestic abuse sucks. It's a cycle."

While the talk moved on to less interesting business, I remembered the scene at Watertown Airport this morning. After the night's storm, the morning dawned bright and clear. We stood by the gate at the landing strip. The plane was idling on the runway, waiting.

The wind blew gently through Miss Wilsie's platinum hair. Excitement and happiness made her look young, and I could see the ghost of her beauty in her fine bones.

"Well, Marianna, I hope you'll come out and visit us in California," she said, stroking my cheek.

"You know you're welcome anytime," Jamey put in. "We really owe you. And thank you for looking after Grammy."

"I'm gonna miss you, Miss Wilsie," I started mistily, hugging her until I could feel her thin fragile bones through her silk shirt. "It's not gonna be the same without you."

"Well, my dear," she said briskly, "It's going to be better than ever now. Besides, you'll come out and visit us. Just promise me, no more bad news delivering. It can get you into serious trouble, don't you see." She was looking at the plane, not me, so I didn't have to promise no more messengering.

Miss Wilsie had never been one to regret or become sentimental. I could tell in her mind, she was already up in the air, heading for California and her next adventure. A lot of transitioning people were about to be delighted and my life was about to be a little less interesting. "Finn, make sure Marianna doesn't get sucked back into that dreadful job," Miss Wilsie had commanded him.

Finn shook her hand. "I will try, Miss Wilsie, but you can't tell Marianna much." He grinned at her and she winked at him.

"Hey!" I said, half annoyed and half amused. "I'm right here, you know."

They both turned and looked at me as if I were two years old and had just done something cute.

Susan drew me into an embrace. I was pleased to note she smelled like lavender. "Thank you for everything," she said. "You saved my life."

"No, you saved your own life, Susan," I said, although privately, I thought I did a really good job of rescuing her. But you have to be modest.

We grinned at each other.

Sometimes, you don't need words.

Jamey looked at her watch. "Well, darlings, we need to move on. We're flying into the wind, and I'm renting this plane by the hour. Come get a hug, Marianna! You're an amazing woman, and I thank you so much. Please come out. You'll be so pleased when you see how happy I make Grammy. She's going to be the queen of all she surveys. And she'll have a whole new reason to live, trust me."

"I believe you. Just make sure she doesn't take over!"

Jamey grinned. "Finn, thank you. You're welcome to come to California anytime, too. Lots of good blue water sailing in the Pacific."

They shook hands and the little party crossed the tarmac and boarded the small jet. We watched as it revved up and taxied down the runway. I waved as it lifted off, circled west and disappeared into the clouds, waved until I couldn't see the plane anymore.

"Are you crying?" Finn asked,

putting a hand on my shoulder. "No need for that."

"Just a little," I admitted. "And some of it is because I'm happy. I love a happy ending."

Finn nodded. " Now that that's all over, we can get to the business of us," he said, grinning. He put his arm around me and drew me close. "I was afraid to ask you out," he said. "I thought maybe you were put off by the choir."

"Not that. I think that's great. Better than the Church of Angry Jesus. But I thought you and Susan were -- - you know." I gestured vaguely.

"No. Just friends. You and I, we're not kids anymore, just a couple of locals, stuck here on the ground. We may as well make the most of it. Hot, smart women like you are hard to find."

"May as well make the most of it," I smiled.

Finn leaned over and kissed me long and hard. It was every bit as good as I'd imagined it would be.

"We've got all the time in the world for romance, but right now, I could use a cup of strong coffee."

"I love a man who has his priorities straight," I said.

We walked toward the airport café. Out of the corner of my eye, I saw a car pull up to the terminal, and Mrs. Chively, the social worker, jumped out with some papers in her hand. She was closely followed by Fred, looking at lot worse for wear. I had a feeling this was nothing good, but they had no power over us. Miss Wilsie was high in the air, away from the clutches of those who thought they had her best interests and a court order in hand.

They stared, stunned, at the empty sky.

Change, I decided at that moment, might not be all bad.

Chapter Twenty-Three

"So, what now?" Jimmy asked, bringing me back to the Lucky Duck.

I shrugged. "Stu, you're gonna have to write the story up. I can't do it. I can't be impersonal about it. I'm too close to it to be objective."

"I think we can all agree that someone has to write it up," Stu agreed. "And it's going to make one hell of a story, and we're going to break it first!"

"Score!" Jimmy cried, high fiving everyone. "This is big for us!"

That's when I remembered the large manila envelope Miss Wilsie had thrust into my bag as she boarded the jet.

"Wait until I'm in the air to read this, darling," she commanded me. I had barely noticed it at the time.

I reached into my bag and pulled

out the envelope. I'd forgotten all about it until this minute. Well, it had been one hell of a night and day.

I scanned the papers Miss Wilsie'd left me, and then scanned them again. When I still couldn't make sense of what I was reading, I handed them over to the gang. "See what you make of this. I don't get it."

Stu studied the papers over his glasses. His eyebrows went up into his hairline.

"Marianna, do you realize what you have here?" Donna asked.

"Well, girl, you landed in some high cotton." Jimmy's grin split his face from ear to ear.

I shook my head. "Does it say what I think it says?"

Stu nodded. "I think you'd need a lawyer to look this over, but it seems like Miss Wilsie Sharpless has deeded you the house on River Street, and enough money in trust to pay the taxes and maintain it. And a little left over, which she says, she hopes you'll use to further the interests of the *Santimoke Gazette.*"

Jimmy let out a gut-busting roar. "She also says you are not to join her son's Fred's church, or in any other way support them. Because Fred's given them enough of her money."

It sounded like the whole bar was applauding me, but I'm not so arrogant as to think that. Probably, some guy with a ball had done something fantastic on one of the big screen TVs.

"Miss Wilsie, I wish you hadn't," I said, as if she were sitting there.

And as if she were sitting there, I could see her putting her be-ringed hands on her chin and looking at me down the long incline of her majestic nose. Miss Wilsie was not used to having her whim of iron disputed.

"Fred's not gonna like this," I stuttered.

"Oh, everyone in Santimoke County knows Fred has more money than God. He ain't gonna miss a house and a chip of stock. Besides, it looks as if she has it wrapped up all right and tight."

"She hopes you'll use the building to open offices for the Gazette,"

Donna gasped. "This means we'll have a place, a brick and mortar place to produce the paper. We can afford to hire a sales staff and more stringers and photographers and have a real paper!"

I finished my cheeseburger, every greasy bite of it. The celebrations were going on all around me, but I still couldn't believe my good fortune, or the Santimoke Gazette's good fortune. After all, we were a team, and I couldn't do this without my friends and colleagues.

"I think I can pick up the check," I said. "Let's have another beer. Day-um. I can't quite absorb this. Thank you, Miss Wilsie, somewhere in the flyover states!"

We all raised our glasses to Miss Wilsie, our fairy godmother.

I have to say we were all pretty high when we rose from the table, and it wasn't just the beer. It was the sheer exaltation of a happy ending.

Nothing in my experience had prepared me for a happy ending. Mostly, my endings nosedived into crash and burn.

***

That Sunday at Hopkins United Methodist, I sat in the congregation and watched the choir singing "Been in the Storm So Long".

It had been so long since I had been in a church, any church, that I was sure the roof would fall in on me, but it didn't. I have to admit that Finn stood out in the Methodist Men's Praise Chorus. There was no disguising his Irish ancestry up there; he was Honky McWhite. But he blended right in. He had a terrific baritone, he knew how to move and sway and you could tell he was really happy. He had soul. The music got him right where he lived, and everyone seemed to accept that it was good and right that he should be there.

When Finn had the solo, he found me in the congregation and

grinned, and I grinned back, genuinely moved.

This wasn't my first service here and I had a lot of friends in the congregation who welcomed me. And I had a reason to be grateful to God, Whoever She might be. I'd been through the storm and come out on the other side. I raised my hands, palms up, to receive the blessings.

When the spirit moved me, I signified. I may have been raised frozen chosen, but I was at home in the world. If writing had taught me nothing else, it had taught me to be at home wherever I was.

Today's sermon was on gratitude, and I felt grateful.

You just have to have faith, like Finn, like these people here and those people over at Angry Jesus and at every other church in Santimoke County. And faith for all those people whose worship was a cup of coffee and the Sunday funnies. I focused my mind and listened to the sermon and the music. The road ahead might not be smooth, but I was going to tackle it.

As if they'd read my mind, the congregation launched into "Rough Side of the Mountain." I sang along in my uncertain, off key voice.

Finn told me he'd been attracted to the church and the music by a couple of guys who worked in the boatyard and passed the time singing hymns. He was so entranced, they invited him to come to church with them. He tried out for the choir and found his church home. I wasn't sure if it was my church home or even if I had a church home. But here I was.

"You ready to go?" Finn asked, grinning at me as he wrapped his arm around my shoulders at the end of the service.

I put my head on his shoulder, happy and slightly goofy, maybe as much with happiness as contentment.

"Some good deeds do go unpunished," Finn said. " Come on. Marianna. Let's go home."

Acknowledgements

Thanks to Karen Basile, who did the initial reading, proofing and provided valuable feedback. Thanks to Ed Chappell for his constant support. And I am eternally grateful to Cheril Thomas, who proofed, did layout and formatting and worked her magic to bring this book into shape for Kindle and Createspace, dragging me into the 21st Century.

About the Author

Helen Chappell lives and writes on the Eastern Shore of Maryland where she tries to keep a low profile and stay out of the line of fire. She has covered the Eastern Shore for the *Washington Post* and the *Baltimore Sun*. She is the author of forty-two books including *The Oysterback Tales,* the *Sam and Hollis* mystery series and *The Chesapeake Book of the Dead.* Enjoy her monthly column about life on the Eastern Shore in the *Tidewater Times.*

Made in the USA
Middletown, DE
12 March 2023

26645797R00144